"Love costs too much. I want no part of it."

"Adele, love has *given* you so much," Mac countered, hating to see her so distraught. He brushed his hand against her cheek before quietly continuing, "You and your foster sisters have two aunts that adore you. And you have each other to lean on."

"True," she agreed solemnly, her gaze holding his.

"But?" Mac hated that she couldn't seem to break free of her past.

"This sounds a little schoolgirlish, but I've always longed to have somebody who loved me enough that I never doubted it."

"I don't count?" Mac arched his brows.

"You were my best friend, Mac, and that counts for a lot. But you never loved me," she said. "Not romantically. We're just friends."

"Just friends." His mouth turned down. "Friendship's not enough now?"

"It's a great deal, Mac, and I will always treasure it." Her hand closed around his and squeezed it. "But my escape from the past was always a dream about a fairy-tale love that would override my past." She withdrew her hand. "Hasn't happened and I doubt it ever will."

Lois Richer loves traveling, swimming and quilting, but mostly she loves writing stories that show God's boundless love for His precious children. As she says, "His love never changes or gives up. It's always waiting for me. My stories feature imperfect characters learning that love doesn't mean attaining perfection. Love is about keeping on keeping on." You can contact Lois via email, loisricher@gmail.com, or on Facebook (loisricherauthor).

Books by Lois Richer

Love Inspired

Rocky Mountain Haven

Meant-to-Be Baby
Mistletoe Twins

Wranglers Ranch

The Rancher's Family Wish
Her Christmas Family Wish
The Cowboy's Easter Family Wish
The Twins' Family Wish

Family Ties

A Dad for Her Twins
Rancher Daddy
Gift-Wrapped Family
Accidental Dad

Visit the Author Profile page at Harlequin.com for more titles.

Mistletoe Twins

Lois Richer

HARLEQUIN® LOVE INSPIRED®

Recycling programs
for this product may
not exist in your area.

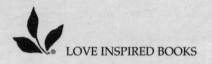

LOVE INSPIRED BOOKS

ISBN-13: 978-1-335-50993-2

Mistletoe Twins

Copyright © 2018 by Lois M. Richer

www.Harlequin.com

Printed in U.S.A.

And we know that all things work together for good to them that love God, to them who are called according to his purpose.
—*Romans* 8:28

This book is dedicated to my mom,
who always believed God had an answer
for whatever problems came her way.

Chapter One

"Are we there yet?"

"Yes. This is The Haven." Adele Parker pulled up in front of the big stone house set in the foothills of the Canadian Rockies and heaved a sigh of pure happiness. "We're home."

"Can we get out now?" In the back seat Francie nudged her brother, Franklyn, awake. "I'm tired of riding in this car."

"Me, too," agreed her four-year-old twin, with a yawn. "Tired."

"It *was* a long drive from Edmonton." Adele twisted to smile at the pair, treasuring the way their little faces came alive with interest at their first view of this place she loved. "Let's get out but zip your jackets first. The mountain winds will be chilly." Not wanting to arrive home disheveled, she checked her makeup, patted her curls, then thrust her arms into her own coat before exiting the car.

"Hey, where's the snow?" Francie looked around, obviously disappointed.

"An' where's the ski hill you tole us 'bout?" Franklyn frowned. "This is a desert, like in that story you read us."

"Franklyn, that's not true," Adele scolded. "Deserts

don't have all those green spruce trees, do they? Anyway, it's barely October. It's not time for winter yet. But don't worry, snow will come." She smothered a chuckle at their glum looks, then hunkered down beside Franklyn and pointed north. "The ski slopes at Jasper are about an hour away. In those mountains. Maybe we'll go there one day, hmm?"

"Okay." Usually biddable, Franklyn assessed The Haven. "It's a very big house. And it is, too, made of stone. Francie said it wasn't," he confided to Adele.

"I won't ever lie to you, Franklyn." A thrill whispered through Adele at the trust in his dark eyes. Trust in *her*.

"It's kinda like the castle in *Beauty and the Beast*." Francie leaned back so far Adele worried she'd topple backwards. "Is it cold in there, Delly?" Their nickname for Adele brought back fond memories of her own youth at The Haven.

"No. It's warm and friendly and the best place on earth." *It's home.* "C'mon. I'll show you." Grasping each child's hand, she led them to the side of the house, in through the back door and into her favorite room, the kitchen.

"Adele!" Her aunties—Margaret and Tillie Spenser—sat at the massive kitchen table having tea, just as Adele had expected. Tillie was pouring while Aunt Margaret snuck a wafer from the stack on a plate.

"We didn't hear you arrive." Margaret jumped up and hugged her so tightly Adele could barely breathe—and she loved it. "We're so glad you've come home, dear."

"Thank you. I'm so glad to be here." She should have come back right after her breakup with Rafe, Adele mused as Tillie's embrace followed, just as tight, just as welcome.

The elderly women bent to study the twins. "Who have we here?" Tillie asked.

"I'm Francie. An' this is my brother, Franklyn, an' that's Delly—"

"They already know me, sweetie." Adele helped the children shed their coats. "These are my foster aunties." She introduced them.

"How come you have—" Francie paused in her usual litany of questions when someone rapped on the door.

"This is a busy place." Tillie hurried to welcome their guest. "Mac, dear! I didn't know you were home."

Adele whirled around, thrilled to see the man who'd been her best friend since the day she'd arrived at The Haven with her three foster sisters more than twelve years ago.

"Mac McDowell!" She hurried forward and wrapped him in a hug. Her heart dropped when her very best friend eased away a little too quickly. That was when she noticed how his coat sleeve hung empty from the elbow down. She gulped and refocused. "It's good to see you, Mac."

"Good to see you too, Delly." Mac's easy smile flashed. Then he stepped around her to greet Tillie and Margaret.

"Hey, you said Delly." Franklyn studied him curiously. "That's our name for Adele."

"It was mine before it was yours." In a quick sleight of hand Mac, who'd always adored kids, produced two candies from behind their necks that he then offered to them.

Adele introduced the twins, then asked, "How did you know I was home, Mac?"

"I didn't. Dad sent me to talk to your sister. He says Victoria wants our stables to offer a trail ride business." He shrugged. A wry smile played with his lips. "Dad doesn't think the Double M can handle it, mostly I think because he feels overwhelmed by the ranch these days. But apparently she's been insistent so he wants me to refuse her. I'm guessing Victoria's still very, uh, strong-minded?"

"We call it determined," Margaret agreed, eyes dancing. "That's why we're happy to have her running The Haven for us—"

"I'm sorry, Mac," Tillie interrupted her sister. "You've missed her. Things have changed around here. Victoria is married now, to Ben Adams. They've adopted Ben's nephew Mikey and they have a daughter, baby Grace."

"Yes, and today, while Mikey's at school," Margaret continued, "Victoria, Ben and Grace are spending some family time together in Chokecherry Hollow." She smiled. "They won't be back from town till after school. But please join us for tea. Or coffee, if you prefer."

"Thank you." Looking somewhat confused by all the information, Mac shrugged out of his sheepskin coat and hung it on a peg by the door. "I'd love some coffee."

As she'd done a hundred times before, Adele automatically pulled the coffee canister from the fridge and started the brewer. She also made fresh tea for the aunties and, at their request, but a little hesitantly, selected two china teacups and saucers for the twins.

Adele deliberately waited until everyone was seated at the table and the aunts were busily engaged in explanations to the twins about the proper way to drink their tea-flavored milk from fancy china.

Under the cover of their conversation she murmured, "Want to tell me what happened with your arm, Mac?"

"Lost half of it after I crashed my plane. I didn't think the ground was quite so close. Some test pilot, huh?" The indifferent shrug and quirky lopsided grin that had been Mackenzie McDowell's trademark since the day he'd pulled Adele's hair in fourth grade now lifted the corner of his mouth. "Since everything below my elbow was amputated I can't fly anymore." He shrugged in apparent nonchalance. "I need to figure out a new way to earn my living."

That was typical Mac. Play down his pain and suffering. Except Adele could see fine white lines at the edges of his glacial-green eyes and etched deep around his mobile lips. She knew he still suffered. She also noted that he gave few details about his accident. Because he was still in pain or because he'd done something wrong? She wanted to hear the whole story, but she'd wait until he was ready to tell her.

"I'm very sorry," she whispered as she squeezed his hand.

"Thanks." Mac immediately withdrew his hand. "Oh, wait." He rose and walked to the door. He leaned out to grab something and returned with a handful of bedraggled and grubby—what?

"Uh, thanks. I think." Adele accepted his offering gingerly. "What are they?"

"No clue, but Mom said your aunts could use them." Mac made a face but this time he wasn't pretending. Adele knew all about his mother's propensity for inventing recipes to use what most people considered weeds. "Herbs?" he suggested.

Not like any herbs I've ever seen.

"Maybe." Adele studied the stalks dubiously. "I'll set them on the window ledge until we're ready to use them." *Which will be never.*

Gingerly she laid the bundle down, recalling a long-ago potluck at Chokecherry Hollow's First Avenue Church, a white-steepled building in the little Alberta town five miles away. The entire membership had become ill from eating Mrs. McDowell's "open range" salad.

Not going to happen in my kitchen. When she lifted her

head, Mac was studying her with a look that said he knew she hadn't a clue what the stalks were for.

"Don't tell your mom I didn't recognize her herbs, okay?" Adele begged. "I'll figure it out eventually."

"Or you'll make up some crazy name for them like you did for that science experiment we did in Mr. Burnder's sixth grade class. Esponsidonia, wasn't that what you called that oozing pink gunk that spilled out of our volcano?" He tilted his handsome head to one side and asked, "How come you were the only one who didn't get spattered by it?"

"Because I moved out of the way." She blushed when he hooted with laughter.

"Oh, the times I tried to get some dirt on you." Mac shook his head, his smile lingering. "Never seemed to work. Two seconds later you were back to polished perfection, even then."

"I like clean and tidy," she defended.

"I know, kiddo." Mac's empathetic smile said explanations weren't needed. He'd never needed them; he always seemed to understand her. "So what are you making for dinner tonight, Chef Adele?"

"I—um, don't know. I didn't intend to—er, start cooking until tomorrow." Why was she bumbling? She'd known Mac for eons. They'd been besties all through school and never once had she felt awkward, so why now? "How's your coffee?"

"I haven't tasted it yet." Mac thrust his gleaming black cowboy boots in front of him then glanced from the cup to her before wrinkling his nose. "It's not made with tree roots or something, is it?"

"Just coffee, mountain grown," she assured him, chuckling as he took a timid sip. "See?"

"Excellent. As usual." Mac grinned. "By the way, I believe all coffee's mountain grown."

"Except your mother's." Adele burst out laughing when he rolled his eyes, just as she'd expected.

Mac was always fun. She'd missed him, missed this. Sharing, laughing, friendship. The connection they'd had—Adele had never managed to find that bond with another man, though she'd certainly tried. She'd dated men from her church, even become engaged to Rafe, which turned out to be a colossal mistake when she finally realized they were miles apart when it came to goals and aspirations. Now she realized she'd never found the same bond with Rafe as she'd always known with Mac.

If only she'd fallen in love with someone like her best friend.

Adele pushed away the silly thought. As if there was anyone else out there like Mac. She smiled when the twins burst into laughter at Aunt Tillie's comment. A deep sense of fulfillment settled inside her at this return to The Haven. The familiar kitchen, the orderly row of cooking tools she'd long ago coaxed the aunties to buy, memories of the savory smells she'd always loved to create—she'd done the right thing in quitting her job and bringing the twins to The Haven. They deserved a home and she was going to give these two orphans just that. Contrary to Rafe's criticism, she *could* be a single mom, and she would do it without him. Wasn't that what God wanted?

"Delly, can we go with these aunties?" Francie jerked her arm to get her attention. "They gots some 'puter games."

"Aunt Margaret certainly does have lots of fun games. Go ahead and behave. I'll be here if you need me." She patted the little girl's shoulder and smiled encouragement at her less boisterous brother. When they'd left, she faced Mac. "So?"

"You tell me," he said, one sandy eyebrow quirked upward. "How is it to be home again? For good?"

Mac watched Adele's face, confused by the—how to describe it?—lack of sparkle in those amber eyes.

"I'm home for a while and it feels very good. I'm fostering those two sweethearts." Adele glanced at the retreating twins and then at him, but there was hesitation as she explained, "And I'm considering adoption." He couldn't quite decipher her expression.

"Your fiancé wants that?" Mac sipped his coffee while trying not to show his dismay. He'd always supported Delly. That wasn't going to change.

"I don't have one." Adele grimaced. "I told you a long time ago that I was never going to marry and repeat my parents' disasters."

"Apparently you forgot that vow because you *did* get engaged, Delly. The aunts wrote me about it a while ago." He saw pain in those expressive eyes. "What happened?"

"What always happens with romance, what I've been avoiding my entire life." She squeezed her eyes closed and sighed. "Arguments."

"About?" *Don't prejudge the guy.* Mac waited for her to explain.

"Rafe and I argued about pretty much everything, but recently they centered around Francie and Franklyn. He said I was getting too involved." She rolled her eyes.

Mac figured this Rafe couldn't have known Delly very well if he expected her not to get involved with a pair of needy kids.

"We bickered a lot about that, but I thought if he'd just get to know them…" Adele shook her blond head, apparently unwilling to tell Mac all. "One day Rafe informed me that he didn't want a ready-made family. Or any family." She stared at her hands. "I tried to understand. But I couldn't marry him and not care what happened to the twins. I kept praying for God to help."

"I see." Mac frowned but said nothing more, waiting for the rest of the sad story.

"Then Rafe missed an important dinner. He lied about why and I knew it, so I pressed him. People who love each other don't lie to their partners." The way she compressed her lips told Mac she was still hurting. "Turns out Rafe didn't love me, not the way I thought. He wanted to marry me because he figured I'd be an asset to him in his bid for full partner at his law firm. Francie and Franklyn didn't fit his plan."

Mac hissed air between his teeth, disgusted with a man he'd never met. "Ow."

"Yes. Reality bites. Rafe wasn't the man I'd dreamed he was. Our so-called *love* was all in my mind."

Mac could see her struggling not to show her distress over that discovery. Since the day they'd first met, he'd understood that Adele needed to replace the painful memory of her parents' bitter marriage and abusive home life.

"I finally realized that marrying Rafe would be repeating the ugliness of my parents' marriage." She shook her head to emphasize her words. "I won't do that, Mac. I will not subject myself or anyone else to the hate and misery of that. I experienced it as a kid. I'm never going there again. Rafe was the second guy I trusted and then realized didn't really love me."

Mac sat up straight at the news. Delly had loved someone else?

"So I've reaffirmed my decision never to marry," she said firmly. "I don't think I could endure the failure."

"Not necessarily gonna happen," he murmured, but she ignored him.

"You know me and my past. My parents—my childhood dug marks too deep. Even when they were finally splitting up they couldn't agree on parenting, so Gina and I were sent to foster care." She swallowed hard. Seeing her so determined not to cry made Mac feel helpless. "How could they do that to their own kids?"

"I don't know, Del—"

"So-called *love* wreaked havoc with my self-esteem." Adele straightened, control regained. "It was even worse this time to realize Rafe was prepared to pretend to love me, but only as long as I fit the mold he had. Love tore my family apart, Mac. I thought I was over the effects of that, but here I am, reliving the same old feelings. Love costs too much. I want no part of it."

"Adele, love has *given* you so much," Mac countered, hating to see her so distraught. "Tillie and Margaret took you, Victoria, Olivia and Gemma from the foster system before you were teens. The four of you grew up here at The Haven surrounded by so much love from those two ladies that the rest of us local kids envied you." He brushed his hand against her cheek before quietly continuing. "You and your foster sisters have two aunts that adore you. And you have one another to lean on."

"True," she agreed solemnly, her gaze holding his. "And we love that the aunties did that for us."

"But?" Mac hated that she couldn't seem to break free of her past.

"This sounds a little schoolgirlish, but I've always longed to have what other girls had," she whispered. "Boyfriends, somebody who loved me enough that I never doubted it."

"I don't count?" Mac arched his brows.

"You were my best friend, Mac, and that counts for a lot. But you never loved me," she said. "Not romantically. We're just friends."

"Just." His mouth turned down. Adele had been a huge part of his life before he'd left home. Was he going to lose all that? "Friendship's not enough now?"

"It's a great deal, Mac, and I will always treasure it." Her hand closed around his and squeezed it. "But my escape from the past was always a dream about a fairy-tale love that would override my past." She withdrew her hand. "Hasn't happened and I doubt it ever will."

"That's why you went out with Kent Krane from high school." He gaped when she nodded. "I always wondered what you saw in him."

"Kent was handsome enough to be a Prince Charming, but he wasn't for me." She smiled sadly. "Before I met Rafe, after Jeff dumped me—"

"Jeff?" Mac frowned.

"A guy from my church in Edmonton." Adele sighed. "I dated several. I'd pray about those dates, wait for God to stop me or let me know those men weren't *the* one. When He didn't, I'd go out for coffee with them. Or lunch. Or to adult fellowship. Whatever." She couldn't read Mac's expression, but she was pretty sure he thought she was an idiot. "None of them fit my list."

"Until Rafe." He waited for her nod. "Let me guess. He was attentive, he was fun and he made your heart speed up."

"Yes, all of it." She thrust out her chin when he smiled. "What's wrong with that?"

"Nothing if he was the one. But he wasn't. Can I take a stab at guessing why?"

"I already told you why. But go ahead." Adele looked as if she wished she'd never told him anything.

"Don't take this the wrong way, but you, dear friend Adele, *like* perfection. Never a hair out of place, even when you're cooking full tilt. Your chef's whites are probably always pristine, right?"

"I try," she acknowledged. "So what? You're making me sound as if I'm suffering from obsessive-compulsive disorder," she complained.

"No, I'm not saying that at all." Mac paused.

While recuperating after the amputation, he'd had sessions with a psychotherapist, during which Mac had talked about Adele, a lot. It had helped him avoid facing his own truth. The therapist had offered insights that helped Mac understand much more about her and about his friendship with her. Maybe he should shut up now, but Delly was his friend and he wanted to help her.

"What are you saying, Mac?" she demanded in a testy tone.

"Sweetie, you were a kid who lived in a place of turmoil. Everybody deals with things differently. After my brother died, I rode broncs, the worst ones. I needed to feel like I was challenging life."

"You were." Adele tossed him a cheeky grin.

"Agreed. *You* coped with your messed-up world by learning to bring order from chaos. Once you had things in order, perfect, you were able to deal with them."

"I guess." At least she was listening.

"Delly, I think it's the same in your love life. You're looking *for* perfection." Mac met her glare head-on. "I mean that sincerely. Even today, after a long car ride with two active kids, you look as if you stepped off a magazine page." He grinned as a thump sounded from the depths of the house. "The kids did, too, though I doubt they do now."

She rolled her eyes.

"What I'm trying to say is that there's no man alive

who could get a perfect grade from you." He immediately wished those words unsaid.

"That's not very nice, Mac," she snapped, making her sound cold, the pain in her eyes telling Mac that he'd gone too far. And Adele Parker was anything but cold. "I only told you that so that you'd understand why I am no longer considering marriage."

"You couldn't maybe consider living with less than your dream of husband perfection?" he teased, striving for a little lightness. When she shook her head, he sighed. "So instead you'll settle for single parenthood." Mac squeezed his eyes closed, then sighed. "I give up."

Adele didn't like Mac saying he gave up on her. But she didn't have time to think about it before his next question.

"What's the news on your sister?" he asked.

"There isn't any." Adele sighed with frustration before explaining, "As you know, Gina went to a foster home like me. After that, it's as if she disappeared. No one in the foster system can or will tell me anything. I'm beginning to wonder if I'll ever find her."

"You will." Mac sounded confident.

"God willing." She wanted to see Gina so badly. God didn't want her to marry but didn't He want her reunion with Gina?

"How did you get involved with Francie and Franklyn?" Mac asked.

"After Victoria had baby Grace I guess my maternal instinct kicked in. I never realized how much I love kids until I held Grace. I was already involved with the Big Sister program, but little Grace got me interested in foster parenting, just on weekends mostly. Or overnight. That's how I met the twins. They stole my heart."

"I can understand that. They're quite the pair." Mac smiled.

"Since marriage isn't an option, I've decided to build my family by adoption while I keep searching for Gina." She held her breath, hoping for his approval.

But Mac frowned. "Um, Adele—"

"Please don't lecture me how I'm going about it all wrong, Mac. How I need to be married to have kids, how a man should be part of the twins' lives." Adele made a face. "People always say that's God's ideal plan, and given the perfect partner, I'd agree. But I haven't found him, and life is moving on."

"We're the same age. We're not old!" Mac's protest made her smile. "Are we?"

"No," she said gently. "But it's not about you and me, Mac. Those two sweet kids lost their parents in a car accident. They don't have a mom and a dad anymore." The usual bubble of anger built inside her. "They're growing up being shuffled from one crowded foster home to the next. That's not right. Francie and Franklyn can't wait for my Prince Charming to show up."

If Mac was surprised by her passion, he didn't show it. He simply waited for her to continue.

"I'd go to the foster care office and keep seeing Francie's and Franklyn's sad little faces as they waited to be shunted to their next home." She pursed her lips. "Do you know what their foster parents complained about most?"

Mac frowned, shook his head.

"That they're too wild. That was one of Rafe's issues, too." She wrinkled her nose at the memory, then continued. "They're just normal, active, healthy kids who need some time and attention." She thrust out her chin. "I'm going to give them that and lots of love."

"Good for you." Mac sounded sincere.

Somehow Adele hadn't expected that acceptance. "Thank you."

Unnerved by his intense scrutiny and the way it made her stomach do odd dances it had never done before, Adele shifted her gaze to the big kitchen window overlooking their valley. The late-afternoon sun sinking behind the not-too-distant peaks of the Canadian Rockies turned the sky into a wild profusion of oranges, reds and purples that seemed full of possibility.

That was why she'd come back to The Haven. For the possibility of having a family to love.

"Are you really okay about your breakup, Delly?"

"Totally." She faced him, her heart thudding with pleasure at the sight of that familiar, tousled beach-bum-blond hair. "I'm so glad you're back, Mac," she said quietly. "I've missed you."

"Because your beau is gone?" His mouth spread wide in a teasing grin.

"No. Because you've always been my best friend. I doubt you've missed me, though." She studied his face. "You haven't texted or emailed in ages."

"No." Mac met her stare with a blank look, then changed the subject. "Dad said there have been a lot of foster kids staying here lately."

"He didn't explain? That's my foster aunties' newest ministry. That's why I'm here." Seeing his confusion, Adele clarified, "Tillie and Margaret had this genius idea that The Haven could become a temporary refuge for troubled foster kids. They decided this big old house with its attached grounds, cabins and acres of forest were perfect for it, so they convinced Victoria to become managing director of their new outreach. It's really taken off."

"Those ladies just can't stop being missionaries, can they? Not even after retiring from the mission field, raising you four foster girls or ministering through their let-ter writing campaign to folks serving in the military. And that's not mentioning all their church work." He shook his head. "Not exactly a quiet retirement."

"I doubt the aunties will ever stop being missionaries," Adele said fondly.

"I was the recipient of a few of their letters while I was flying, you know. Their ability to encourage and inspire is amazing." Mac's eyes softened, his voice affectionate. "I admire the ladies for starting another undertaking in what—their seventies?"

"Seventy-five, but Aunt Tillie and Aunt Margaret won't let age stop them. Now that Vic's on board she's pushing to add even more activities, which I'm guessing is why she suggested trail rides to your dad." She glanced around. "I'm here to handle the kitchen end of the operation."

"Good for you, Delly," he cheered.

"We'll see." Adele pushed the plate of wafers toward him. "Store-bought, I'm afraid, but help yourself." As he eagerly grabbed three she said, "Hey, if you're going to be around for a while, you can be the official taste tester for my baking." Maybe then Mac would explain his plans.

"I happen to be extremely good at tasting baking, es-pecially if it's not from Mom's kitchen." He chuckled at her grimace. "What's the pay for an official taste tester, Chef Adele?"

"Food. And you can use me as a reference." She liked the way his smile lit up his whole face. Mac didn't just nod like Rafe did while he continued with his own thoughts. Mac really listened. "You're back to take over the Double M." His face altered so she added uncertainly, "That's the plan, isn't it?"

"Once it was." Mac swept the crumbs off the place mat

and into his napkin, but his expression gave away little. "The parents certainly think their ranch is where I belong."

"You don't?" She blinked in surprise at his diffident response.

"The ranch, especially the stables, was always Carter's dream." His face tightened. When Carter, his elder brother, had died over ten years ago from brain cancer, Adele had comforted Mac through his loss. "I haven't quite figured out my future, Delly."

"But you *are* finished with the military?"

Mac McDowell had been the talk of nearby Choke-cherry Hollow when, in the middle of his second year of college, he'd deserted his agricultural studies for the military. Now he was home again.

"Well, I'm back on the ranch." Mac's lips pinched tight before he forced a grin on his handsome face. His words made it sound like nothing had changed.

But Adele wasn't so sure that was true. Today everything felt different. Her bestie didn't seem the same and it wasn't only because Mac had lost part of his arm. She had a strange feeling that he needed her help, though she wasn't sure with what or that he would even accept it.

"So now what, Mac?" she pressed.

Chapter Two

Exactly. *Now what?*

Mac had no clue. That was why he'd come to The Haven today. He'd hoped to talk to Adele's aunts, to seek their advice about finding God's plan for his future. The army chaplain had insisted He had one, but if so, Mac couldn't figure it out.

"Hey, pal. Did I say something wrong?" Adele's perfect heart-shaped face scrunched up with concern, golden brows drawn together.

"No, I'm just not sure what comes next for me. Mom and Dad have talked for years about taking a cruise to Australia. They're hinting that I could run the ranch, decide if I want to do it permanently, while they're away." His eyes darkened. "I want them to go. Dad's heart isn't great. I know it's the stress of the ranch. They deserve a holiday. But…"

Mac hated the uncertainty in his voice. It sounded like weakness and he despised being weak almost as much as he despised himself for not owning up to his mistake, the one that caused his accident, the one that cost…

"You don't feel well enough to take over?" Adele

frowned. "How long ago was the crash, Mac? No one told me about it or I'd have come to see you."

"I didn't want visitors."

When she blinked at his harsh tone Mac forced himself to relax. Adele had always tried to fix things. For everyone. She didn't know that what he'd done was unfixable and, if he wasn't careful, with her intuition she might learn the truth about his accident. Mac did not want that.

"The crash happened months ago, Delly, and it was a long, hard recovery. It's a good thing you didn't see how bad a patient I was," he teased, then quickly changed the subject. "Anyway, it's your own fault you didn't hear. You've been living it up in Edmonton. Everyone in town is raving about your success, Madame Chef."

"Catering for the bigwigs and all their corporate parties was fun," Adele agreed. "But after breaking up with Rafe—" She shrugged as if it didn't matter, but there was a glint in those eyes that told Mac differently. "It was time to move on. Anyway, I want to be part of this new work at The Haven. But we were talking about you."

"Not much to say." Now he was the one pretending. "I lost my hand and part of my arm when I crashed because I took stupid, reckless chances. I deserve what I got." *Dave didn't.* He shook off the guilty despair that always hovered. "At least my brain still works. Mostly."

"Stop doing that, will you?" No surprise, Adele wasn't buying his pretense. "We've been friends a long time, Mac. Even though we've been out of touch for a while, I can still tell when you're not okay. Tell me what's really bothering you."

"Bossy as ever, aren't you?" But he couldn't lie, not with always-tell-the-truth Delly. "I guess I'm afraid to take over the ranch."

"Got that. Why?"

"It's taking me a while to come to terms with not flying again, not feeling that rush of excitement." Mac knew his response wouldn't end her questions and it wasn't the whole truth, but he couldn't possibly tell her everything. "Ranching now seems pretty tame compared to flying."

"Tame? You always loved ranching." Adele frowned, obviously trying to understand. "Chokecherry Hollow's rodeo starts next week. Granted it's not the world's largest, but you never met a rodeo you didn't enter."

"I can't ride anymore, Delly." He moved his stump.

"Why not?" As kids, she'd always played tough guy, countering his excuses with perfect logic, just like now. "You never needed two hands to ride broncs before, Mac. I distinctly remember you telling me it was all in the legs."

"I'm still healing from my injuries," he quipped, hating this defensive feeling.

"Making ranching *and* riding impossible?" Frowning, Adele leaned forward to peer into his eyes. "Impossible has never been in *your* vocabulary, McDowell. What's the real reason you don't want to stay on the Double M?"

She knew him too well. Mac took a moment to admire the glossy sheen of her golden hair, left free for once so it could cascade past her shoulders in a tumble of curls that was neither messy nor unkempt. No matter what she was doing, Adele always looked perfectly put together.

"I'm not the same person I was when we left high school, Delly," he warned softly.

"Who is?" she shot back. "Life's changed you as much as it's changed me. But at heart we're the same people God created." Her bright amber eyes shone. She looked and sounded so confident in her faith.

Why wasn't he?

"'S'cuse me." The little girl, Francie, stood in the doorway. But neither she nor her brother behind her looked happy.

"What is it, sweetie?"

The little girl launched herself into Adele's arms. "I don't wanna stay here, Delly," she wailed.

Though slightly chagrined that his special moniker for his bestie had been usurped by these two mini-heartbreakers, Mac's annoyance quickly metamorphosed into a rush of compassion as the girl wept as though her heart would break. He choked up just witnessing her misery.

"Sweetheart, what's wrong?" Adele swung Francie onto her knee and wrapped her other arm around Franklyn. "You tell me, Franklyn," she prodded when Francie couldn't stop sobbing.

"Those aunties said we hafta have different rooms." A hint of anger underlay Franklyn's glowering expression. "Francie don't want to."

Adele lifted her head and shrugged at Mac helplessly. The shimmering glow of mother love in her beautiful eyes made him gulp.

"Where *do* you want to sleep, Francie?" she asked.

"Me an' Franklyn like sharin'." Francie sniffed and rubbed her eyes. "When the bad dreams c-come—" And there she went again, bawling her heart out. Mac felt utterly helpless, and he hated it.

"Sweetheart, did the aunties say you *had* to have two rooms?" Adele gently smoothed away Francie's tears, smiling when the child shook her head. "Then you're crying because you think they'll make you?"

"I guess." Francie sniffed, then frowned when Tillie and Margaret appeared, slightly out of breath. "Won't they?"

"Of course not. Why didn't you tell them what you wanted?" Adele asked gently.

"We're not s'posed to make a fuss." Franklyn's grave tone made Mac blink. Adele was alert, too. He could tell she was fighting off her annoyance because her back suddenly straightened as it always had when they were in school and someone had irritated her.

"It's not a fuss to say if you don't want to do something, Franklyn," he intervened to give Adele a moment to regroup. "Otherwise, how will people know what you want?"

"But the lady at that office where we go said we gotta—Ow!" Franklyn rubbed his arm and glared at Francie. "She pinched me."

"She's going to apologize," Adele promised with a reproving glance at Francie. "But first I need to say something to both of you and I want you to listen very carefully."

Mac had to stifle a chuckle at the uh-oh look filling Francie's face.

"This is The Haven. It isn't like other places you've stayed before. It's different." Adele had to see their skepticism because Mac sure did.

He was also very aware of Tillie and Margaret standing in the doorway, worried and probably praying for the two waifs. But Delly was right. The Haven was like no other place on earth.

"Here you may ask for whatever you need. You won't ever get in trouble for asking. You may not always get what you ask for, but we can't help you if you don't ask." Adele continued, gently but firmly, "And you don't have to be afraid here. We love you both and we're all going to do everything we can to make sure you're happy. Okay?"

Franklyn nodded but it seemed Francie wasn't quite convinced.

"C'n Franklyn an' me sleep in the same room an' c'n it be blue, light not dark, an' c'n we have lotsa toys 'n' everything?" she asked in a rush.

"Hmm, let's see." Adele's face glowed as she glanced at Mac. "Yes, yes, yes and maybe. Okay?"

"Uh-huh." Clearly shocked, Francie stared at Franklyn as if to ask if he believed it.

"Good. An apology?" She waited, one eyebrow arched as the little girl asked her brother's forgiveness and, receiving it, hugged him. "Now, do you have any other questions, or should we get our things from the car and begin unpacking?" Adele noted Francie's grin at her brother. "What's that look about?"

"C'n me 'n' Franklyn have some candy?" the little girl asked, eyes sparkling with fun.

"Not before supper." Adele rolled her eyes at Mac. "Always a test. Jackets on, children. Let's get busy. But first—"

She didn't have to admonish twice. Francie walked over to the aunties and smiled.

"I'm sorry," she said quietly. "I din't know. Thanks for lettin' us stay here."

"Child, you're very welcome." Tears welled in Tillie's eyes as she brushed her hand against Francie's blond pigtails. "Such pretty hair, just like our Adele's."

"Two more children in the house. How lovely." Margaret clasped her hands together as she thought it through. "We have a pretty blue room with two beds and a wonderful window seat made just for stories. Will that do?"

The children nodded eagerly. Tillie couldn't seem to help smoothing Franklyn's curly hair, to no avail, in Mac's opinion.

"See how easy that was?" Adele chided the children. "Come on now. Time to get busy."

Jackets on, they hurried out the door, but Mac hung back.

"Dear boy, I do hope you'll be dropping by frequently now that both you and Adele are home," Tillie enthused.

Immediately enveloped in a cloud of scent Delly had once informed him was the aunts' favorite lemon verbena, Mac felt like he had come home.

"Thank you. Have you been skiing, Tillie? I'm envious of your tan." Other than the tan, the identical twin sisters were almost impossible to tell apart.

"Everyone's envious, dear. Especially Margaret, though she won't try a bottled tan. I love it." Tillie's face saddened. "I'm so sorry about you and your copilot's injuries. We've been praying for you both."

"Er—thank you." He gulped. He hadn't responded to their letters. So how did the aunts know about Dave? And what else did they know? Did they know Mac had caused his buddy's wounds? Did they know he'd never told the truth about the crash?

"If there's any way we can help, dear, you have only to ask," Margaret said, patting his shoulder.

"Well—" He exhaled. "I would like to speak to the two of you privately at your convenience. I need some advice."

"We'd be pleased to help." Margaret smiled. "Shall we text you with a suitable time?"

"Thank you." Mac blinked. The two of them texted. Why was he surprised? No one could call the Spenser sisters old-fashioned. "That would be great."

"Fine. Now, sister, we'd better help our family move in." Tillie chuckled. "Oh, I love the sound of that word. *Family.* Want to help?" she asked Mac brightly.

"Of course." Mac held their coats, then ushered them outside, ensuring they carried only the lightest of items. He'd made his third trip in when the grandfather clock in the hall chimed. He froze.

"Something wrong?" Adele, arms loaded with boxes, stopped short.

"The time. I told Mom I'd only be gone ten minutes and

it's been over an hour." Mac set down his load. "Sorry, but I have to get home. See you later everyone."

"Come for a meal anytime," Adele offered as she walked him to his truck.

"Like I'd miss an opportunity to eat your cooking," he scoffed. "Not a chance, Delly." He lowered his voice. "I'm just wondering, is Francie and Franklyn's stay here unlimited? There's no chance they'll be removed?"

Mac could have kicked himself when a little voice piped up, "Me an' Franklyn are stayin' with Delly forever."

Francie stood behind him, blond pigtails reminding Mac of a very determined Adele when she'd first arrived at The Haven with her three foster sisters.

"Good," he said, with a smile, wishing he'd made sure his questions couldn't be overheard.

"Delly said we might get 'dopted. That means get a fam'ly," she explained. She tilted her head to one side, studying him. "Maybe Delly will 'dopt you, too, Mr. Mac."

Wondering if he looked like he needed Adele to care for him and oddly attracted by the thought, Mac chose his words carefully.

"Call me Mac, okay? No *Mister*." He smiled at them. "It was very nice to meet you, Francie, and you, Franklyn," he added when the boy appeared beside his sister. "I'll see you soon. You, too, Delly. Bye."

He returned Adele's wave but remained still, listening as she reassured the two orphaned kids.

"Mac has his own family, honey." Adele's sweet voice made even Mac feel better.

"Oh." Francie sounded deflated.

"So, he's not gonna be the daddy in our fam'ly?" Franklyn sounded disappointed. "When will we be one?"

"We're already a family, darling, because we're together," Adele assured him. "It's going to take some time

before the judge officially tells us that we can stay together, and things might not go exactly the way we want,
so you'll have to be patient." That was Delly, always telling the truth, painful or not.

Mac watched the kids' faces fall in disappointment and
half wished Adele had shelved her insistence on honesty
for a while, at least until the children had settled in to
The Haven. He also half wished he'd told her the whole
truth about his accident. Because it wasn't going to get
any easier.

"But we don't have to worry about when we'll officially
be a family because God will work that out." With a last
wave at him Adele shepherded the two now-quiet children
and their teddy bears inside.

The back door closed, but for a moment Mac couldn't
move.

God would work it out?

He'd stopped praying a while ago, right after the crash.
Maybe it was coming back to The Haven, maybe it was
hearing the love in Delly's voice as she comforted those
two orphans, or maybe it was their rapt attention to whatever she said. Whatever the reason, a prayer slipped out
of him.

"Please, God, help those kids *and* Adele get their dream
of family."

What about your dream, Mac? What do you want?

Right now, Mac's only dream was to see his good friend
Adele happy. He didn't have a plan for his future. Hopefully Tillie and Margaret would have some advice about
that because Dad couldn't keep running the Double M. *If*
Mac was going to take over, it had to be soon. And if he
wasn't, he owed it to his parents to help sell the place so
they could retire.

But if he didn't ranch, what would he do?

Mac drove home with the same question rolling through his brain that had been there from the moment he'd awakened after the accident.

What's next, God?

Chapter Three

"Anyone who just served that incredible Thanksgiving dinner to more than fifteen people should not look like you do." Three days later, on Monday evening, Mac shook his head at Adele's flawless beauty, then returned his attention to drying the roaster.

"What's wrong with how I look?" From the corner of his eye he saw her pat her chic upswept curls. Then she tugged on his arm and demanded, "Mac?"

"Nothing's wrong with how you look. That's the problem." He chuckled at her confusion, amused by the way she stretched to make herself taller than her actual five foot six. She'd always complained about his eight-inch height advantage.

"Are you laughing at me?" she demanded, brow furrowed.

"I'm amazed at you. After feeding half of Chokecherry Hollow, that dress you're wearing is still immaculate, your eyes sparkle like a fresh batch of your aunt Tillie's Christmas toffee and your cheeks glow like Margaret's Nanjing cherry jelly. You look so good it's scary, Adele."

"Well, I had to make a concession and take off my

heels," she explained. "And I did wear an apron for most of the day, but I'll take that as a compliment, I think."

"That's how I meant it." He ogled the pumpkin pie, felt his stomach protest and shook his head. Today was Monday. Surely Thanksgiving leftovers would still be here tomorrow. He'd better wait. Adele noticed when he patted his midriff and chuckled.

"Aw, don't you feel well, Mac?" Her pseudo look of concern was spoiled by her smirk. "Maybe you shouldn't have eaten all three kinds of pie?"

"This body is a machine," he said proudly, thrusting out his chin. "Burns off calories like a well-oiled engine."

"Uh-huh." Adele had long ago mastered using mere facial expressions to get her point across, and so Mac couldn't help laughing at her mocking mime. But he choked at her next question. "What were you whispering to Francie during dinner?"

"She, uh, asked me if she could tell me about the car accident." Mac focused on drying the last pot as another surge of sympathy for the orphaned children welled inside.

"You'd have a problem with listening?" Adele stretched to place each pan just so on the hanging rack.

"No, but—" Mac frowned. "The kid wants to talk to *me* about the day her parents died. She should talk to a psychologist."

"Both of them already did that. I'm guessing Francie needs to talk more, to you." Adele studied him with a glint of curiosity. "You two seem to have a bond developing. I'm sure Francie would far rather speak to you than a stranger."

"Yes, but what do I know?" Panic filled him. "I might say the wrong thing and hurt her. That's the last thing—"

"Mac." Adele laid her hand on his arm, her voice very gentle. "It's not *what* you say. It's listening to her. Let

Francie vent. Comfort her if she needs it. You know how to do that."

"Because of my accident, you mean?"

"Because you're an expert when it comes to comforting people. I should know. You helped me through some really rough times when we were kids, especially when I first came here." Her faith in him was appealing. "You can do that for Francie, too. She already trusts you. Otherwise why would she have asked you to listen?"

Mac appreciated Adele's assurances, but he had no confidence in himself. He felt broken down, used, a mess up with no prospects for the future. He especially didn't feel good about trying to fill in for Carter, who'd dreamed of putting his own mark on the Double M. Stepping into his dead brother's shoes could hardly be what the chaplain espoused as God's plan for Mac's life.

"I wouldn't know how to help Francie," he demurred, feeling helpless.

"What matters is that you listen," Adele repeated. "If you need a starting point, talk about your miniature horses. The aunts said they're still at the ranch."

"They are but— How long are Francie and Franklyn staying here?" Was it right to get involved if they would be taken away? Was it right not to?

"I wasn't given a timetable. Until I can adopt them, I hope. They have no relatives. They've struggled in several homes because they're normal, active children, which apparently some people don't appreciate." Adele's rolling eyes expressed her thoughts on that. "I'm told most couples want babies or much younger children. Also, sometimes—" She hesitated, glanced over one shoulder.

"Yes?" he prodded.

"Sometimes the twins make up stories," she murmured

very quietly. "It's caused problems for them so we're working on that."

"You believe total and utter truth is always the answer, don't you, Delly?" Mac watched her eyes widen, wondering how she'd react if he told her the truth about his "accident."

"How can relationships grow and how can you trust someone if they're hiding behind lies?" She shrugged. "I think The Haven will be good for the twins even though *I'm* going to be rushed off my feet."

"Because?" He lifted an eyebrow.

"Victoria and the aunts have this place nearly booked solid for the next few months, not only for visiting foster kids but for parties and local events, including a bunch of Christmas festivities. I'm going to need a kitchen helper."

"Don't look at me. Tasting is what I do best. Good thing you have a dishwasher." He grimaced at the dirty dishes still littering the counter. "How will you work with the twins underfoot?" The old protective instinct he'd always felt toward Adele bubbled inside. "You're taking on a lot."

"I'm not sure how anything will work," she admitted as she drained the sink and swished water to clear the suds. "Least of all how it will work with Francie and Franklyn. But I refuse to see those children shuttled from place to place, like I was, like my foster sisters were until the aunts brought us here."

"But—"

"The twins are sweet and loving, Mac." Adele unfolded her spotless apron and set it aside. "They deserve to be able to relax and be kids without worrying about where they'll be sent next."

"Softhearted Delly." He smiled at her feisty attitude. "You always did champion the less fortunate." But there had to be more to her plan. He refilled their coffee then sat down at the table, determined to figure out exactly why his friend was doing this. Thankfully she was in a chatty mood. "Talk to me about this adoption."

She sat and stared into her coffee for several moments.

"You know I had a miserable, abusive childhood. The aunties rescued me from that and brought me here, where there wasn't constant fighting or parents making promises they never kept."

"God used them," he said, loving the way she appreciated all her foster aunts had done.

"For sure." She huffed out a sigh. "Before I left Edmonton this time, I went to see both my parents. I thought maybe there was something I could do to heal the rifts between us, repair the bonds, start new relationships. We are family after all."

"And?" Mac was sorry he'd asked when her face tightened, and her irises darkened.

"They're divorced, haven't lived together for years, have scarcely seen each other in eons. Both have remarried and divorced several times. Yet they're still both miserable, blaming one another, lying about what the other one did to them, full of hate." She shook her head. "I don't want anything like that to touch Francie and Franklyn. They've had enough to deal with, losing their parents."

"Mama Adele, shielding her cubs." Mac savored this fiercely protective side of her.

"The long-held illusion that my parents and I could ever be a family, even a distant one, has finally been irrevocably shattered." Her shoulders went back, her jaw thrust forward. "Now I'm determined to raise Francie and Franklyn with love and support and a solid trust in God's love. On my own, until I can find Gina."

"And if you don't get permanent custody?" Mac felt a responsibility to prepare her.

"I'll hate it," she admitted honestly. "But I'll still do everything I can to make sure they get in to the right home." She studied him intently. "I can't walk away from the twins, Mac. That's not how my aunties raised me."

"I know. That's what I like most about you." He smiled, brushed a tendril off her cheek. "I'll help you however I can." Why did she look so surprised? Hadn't he always been there for Delly? Okay, maybe not lately but— "I care about the twins, too."

"Thank you, Mac." Adele's smile warmed the cold, guilty place inside him.

Would she smile like that, even want him around, if she knew what a jerk he was? She leaned her head against his shoulder for a moment and slid her arm around his waist, hugging him as she'd done so many times before.

"It's so nice to have you back. My dear, dear honest best friend. Home at last."

Mac froze, breathing in the scent of her flowery shampoo, marveling at the soft brush of her silky cheek against his, savoring the gentle intimacy that until this moment he hadn't known he'd missed.

Friend?

Somehow that one expression didn't seem to encapsulate all that he and Adele had shared. It didn't say enough. But since he couldn't come up with an alternative, he slipped his good arm around her and enjoyed the moment, content to remain right where he was. With Adele.

He deliberately ignored that word *honest*. He'd figure the future out later, after he talked with the aunts about God's plan for his life.

Two days after Thanksgiving Adele still blushed at the memory of her sister finding them hugging in the kitchen.

Though she and Mac both knew there'd been nothing romantic in that embrace, Victoria wouldn't let it go.

"You care a lot about Mac, don't you?" she asked now as she sipped her tea at the big kitchen table.

"Mac's my best friend, Vic. Always has been. You know that." Adele checked on the Swiss steak cooking in the oven, added potatoes to bake and a huge dish of rhubarb crisp. "There. Everything should be done in time for supper," she said as she closed the door.

"Where are the twins?" Victoria glanced around.

"With Mac in the aunties' herb garden, checking to see if there's anything left out there that we can still use."

"He sure comes over here a lot—"

"The Haven's gardens had a good yield this year," Adele interrupted, hoping to forestall more of Victoria's questions about Mac. "It was nice to share the excess during the harvest day you organized for those needy families yesterday. Though I doubt the deer are grateful," she added. Maybe her sister's intense dislike of deer wreaking havoc in the garden could change the subject.

Fat chance.

"Is Mac staying to run the Double M?" Victoria ignored Adele's hiss of irritation. "What? I'm just wondering, like everyone else in Chokecherry Hollow."

"And you think I have the answer? I don't know Mac's future plans. I'm not sure he does, either." Adele checked on the French bread she'd set to rise earlier and decided it was ready to form. "If he has decided, he has *not* told me," she added firmly as she greased the bread pans.

"Since when doesn't Mac McDowell talk everything over with you?" Victoria held up both hands at Adele's glare. "Okay, 'nuff said. Except—I'm guessing Mac's the reason you didn't offer me that last piece of pumpkin pie sitting in the fridge. And here I thought our sister bond was strong." Laughing, she strolled out of the room to answer a call from her husband, Ben.

With a grimace directed at her back, Adele shaped the bread into two pans, then began mixing dressing for the coleslaw she'd make when Jake, The Haven's hired man, returned from the cold cellar with one of her aunt's prized cabbages. Finished with her immediate task, she took a moment to savor the aroma-filled kitchen where she'd first learned to cook.

How blessed she'd been to live here with her foster aunts. They'd striven so hard to help her shed her bitterness against parents who'd lied to her about everything, including the visitor to their home that long-ago day, never explaining that she and Gina would be taken into foster care—permanently.

The aunties' love and security had soothed those wounds. That healing love was what she wanted for the twins.

Adele roused from her gloomy thoughts as Mac opened the back door and ushered Franklyn and Francie inside. She loved the sound of the children's laughter, and naturally Mac did everything he could to provoke more of it. It was refreshing to see him so engaged with kids again. In the old days he'd spoken often of his desire for a big family. But he'd mentioned nothing about a girlfriend. Was there now someone special in Mac's world?

She peeked into the pail Mac held out. "Thanks."

"Jake said you can use them. I'd spare you and take these weeds home to my mother but then she'd make something with them and I'd have to eat it." He looked dubious.

"Not weeds. Basil, dill and parsley are always useful in my kitchen." Since Mac's grin did funny things to Adele's stomach, she turned away to rinse the herbs before storing them in a drying dish. "Did you two have fun?"

It was obvious from the children's excited chatter that they had.

"We found punkins," Franklyn exclaimed.

"How many?" Adele asked.

"Tons and tons." Francie waved her hands wildly.

"How many did you find, Francie?" Adele prodded, arching an eyebrow.

"Three," the little girl admitted with a sigh.

"'Nuff so you c'n make punkin pie again?" Franklyn hinted hopefully, then high-fived Mac.

"Because everyone needs more pie right after our Thanksgiving feast?" Adele shot Mac a look, certain he'd come up with that plan.

"Uh-huh. Mac says everybody needs more pie all the time." Franklyn nodded, unabashed.

"Does he?" She angled him a look. "Well, good work finding those pumpkins. Now you two go and wash up. Aunt Tillie and Aunt Margaret are waiting to tell you the next installment of their story about Africa." She watched them leave, a happy glow inside. So far, Adele was loving motherhood.

"They're cute, those two. But they sure keep a guy on his toes." Mac sat down with a sigh and flexed his leg.

"Are you in pain?" Adele studied his face, wondering how she could help.

"No. Just a little stiff. I tried riding this morning." Mac's face gave nothing away.

"Great!" Riding was a sign he was staying, wasn't it? "And?"

"No big deal. Cowboys ride and I am just a cowboy after all." His wink reminded her of a long-ago argument when she'd given vent to her frustration at his show-off tendencies.

"And as you replied, I'm just a cook," she reminded

with a cheeky grin. Then she added, "Of course it's a big deal that you got back on a horse, Mac." Another thought occurred. "Did riding help you decide anything?"

"Adele." His glower scolded her. "I haven't decided anything yet, even though my parents are as eager as you to know if I'll take over running the place. Dad wants to retire."

"I saw him in town. He looked tired," she murmured sympathetically.

"He has to slow down and it's obvious he can't do that as long as they live on the ranch because he won't leave anything to their hired man, who is eminently capable." Mac raked his hand through his sandy-blond hair. "Me—take over the ranch—I don't know." His troubled sigh touched her.

"What concerns you most?" She could at least encourage him to talk about his fears.

"It's a total life change."

"Because you'll miss flying." She nodded.

"It's not just that. You of all people should know that I haven't been the most stable guy in the world. I wasn't very good at after-school jobs, remember?"

"Because you wanted to be on the ranch." She waited, knowing there was more.

"I also dumped college, remember?" His mouth tipped down in a self-deprecating frown. "And I blew my last job. But I'm not sure I'm ready to settle down yet."

"You had to be responsible when you were flying, Mac," she reminded. Something in his expression altered. Was it her reminder about flying? "Anyway, you just said the Double M has a capable ranch manager in Gabe Webber. He knows as much about ranching as your dad. Can't you leave most of the routine stuff up to him? Isn't that why ranchers have hired men?"

"I guess. You make it sound like I don't even really need to be there." Her bestie didn't look at her, so Adele knew there was something else.

"Talk to me, Mac."

"You've changed since you left The Haven, Delly." Those gorgeous eyes of his seemed sad. "You've matured. I'm not sure I have. Not enough."

"Why do you say that?" Surprised to see Mac fiddle with a napkin, she pressed him. "How have I matured? Do I look old?" Her glance in the kitchen mirror produced a laugh from Mac.

"No! But you're more focused, more determined than before. Your plan took a hit with your breakup, but you haven't given up. You're going after a new dream. I don't even have a dream." His grin was wry.

"So dream one."

"I wish I could. It's just—flying is like living life on the edge," he mused aloud, struggling to give words to his feelings. "If things get too boring or too staid I might regret taking on the Double M, or worse, make a mess of it, which will then make my parents ashamed of me."

"Like that would ever happen. They're so proud of you," she praised. "And don't think I have all the answers or any cast-in-stone plans. All I know is I can't give up my motherhood dream." Confused by Mac's now-glowering look she asked, "Tell me about flying your jets. What was it like?"

Immediately his slouch disappeared. His backbone straightened and his shoulders came to attention. His turquoise eyes sparkled with excitement, as if someone had switched on a light inside him.

"Oh, Delly, it's amazing. There's such freedom— nothing's scripted. You have to think fast and improvise to survive. When I'm soaring through the clouds I feel like

I can handle anything. And then I land." Just as suddenly the light in him was snuffed out. "I guess I'm addicted to that adrenaline rush."

"You don't think you'll find that on the Double M?" *Oh, Lord, how can I help him?*

"Maybe I could." He didn't sound convinced. "*If* I hadn't lost my hand or injured my leg."

"Did you feel a thrill like that when you lived here before?" she wondered aloud.

"Sometimes. Mostly at the rodeo or when I was breaking a very stubborn horse." Mac's troubled face sent a pang through her. "Remember how if I got restless I took off to the mountains. If I needed excitement, I'd hike the badlands. Or ski the backcountry. Or climb where tourists never go."

All very risky activities, Adele mentally noted. Was he running *to* or *away* from something?

"I don't have those options anymore," he muttered.

"Mac, you can still ski—"

"I don't want to go to Marmot Basin and stand in line while people gawk at me as I struggle to figure out how to manipulate myself on and off the chair lift with one hand," he interrupted bluntly, his face dark. "I don't want to have to always have someone with me to watch out for me when I white-water raft or climb a rock face. If you want the truth, Delly, if I can't have what I had, I just want to hide." His shoulders slumped. "Maybe the ranch is the best place to do that."

Shocked by the despair in his words and voice, Adele was at a loss. It was no use telling her pal that he'd figure it out or find something else to give him the same high. This was Mac. He'd always gotten his high from life lived on the edge, and now he felt he couldn't.

"I'm sorry. I shouldn't dump my frustrations on you."

His hand covered hers and his gorgeous smile flashed, hiding the loss she'd seen revealed in his eyes mere moments earlier. "Don't worry about me. I'll manage."

"Stop it, Mac." She jerked her hand from under his and rose, facing him as annoyance surged through her. "Stop pretending everything's fine. I can take your honesty. I can't take your fake acceptance of what life has handed you."

To her complete exasperation he laughed.

"What's so funny?" she demanded, hands on hips.

"You and your honesty." Mac shook his head. "Spicy, tart, yet sweet and always, always that blunt demand for honesty. You're the only one who has never let me get away with anything, do you know that, Delly?"

Adele didn't know what to say.

"Remember the night I was going to go hot-rodding and you made me pull over so you could get out?"

"Yes." Adele mostly remembered how maddened she'd been.

"You were always the voice of reason," he said softly, studying her face. "I used to hear your voice sometimes when I was flying."

"No doubt right before you were about to try some silly stunt." She shuddered at the fleeting thought of her world without Mac.

"Sometimes." He looked at his damaged arm. When he spoke next his voice was very quiet, almost as if he were talking to himself. "When I was going down the last time, I could almost hear you chewing me out for—"

"For what?" she nudged, curious to hear. But Mac's face froze. He jerked to his feet.

"I need to get home. I should at least feed my own horses now that I'm back, not leave it to Dad."

"Mac?" Adele waited until he was looking at her. "May

I say something?" She smiled at his slow nod. "You can still do an awful lot, even take chances again, if you must. But maybe now you need to think ahead a bit more, plan it out. Set your goal, calculate the risk and decide if the payoff is big enough."

"Ah, but spur-of-the-moment is half the fun, Delly." His grin returned, as if the old Mac was back, but she knew it was a pretense. Unfortunately he left before she could think of a suitable comeback.

Adele began setting the table, her thoughts in a turmoil. The man was used to riding a roller coaster through life. He'd always thrived on action and if it wasn't there, he'd created it. But Mac was bright, capable and adept at finding unconventional solutions to problems. She didn't think that had changed.

What had changed was Mac's fearlessness. The old Mac would never have cared if someone was watching him or not. He would have charged ahead and done what he wanted, gotten his thrill.

"I'm his friend, so somehow I have to help him see that ranching isn't a dead end, that there's still plenty of opportunity to live an exciting life on the Double M. But how do I do that, Lord?" she asked aloud. Past images of Mac with his precious miniature horses filled her mind. "Maybe I'll start with them."

Francie and Franklyn rushed into the room, raving about their story.

"It was about horses, huh?" *Okay, God, I'm taking that as Your nudge.* "How'd you like to go visit Mac on his ranch tomorrow? Maybe he'll show you his horses. They're just your size."

Entranced by the prospect, the twins accepted the paper and crayons she offered and sat down on the window seat to draw pictures for Mac. When Jake arrived with the cabbage, the kids told him about their planned trip to the ranch.

"You're really good at keeping them busy," he said to Adele. "A born mom."

"Hardly." After Jake left, Adele put the finishing touches on the meal, but his words replayed in her head. Was she going to be a mom? She wanted that, so much.

All at once dreams of *her* children, her *family* gathered here at The Haven, grew full-blown. If she had a daughter, she'd be named Gina, for her sister.

You'll be there for them, but who will be there for you?

Adele pushed away the painful thought. Right now, whatever was wrong, Mac needed her as his friend. She'd concentrate on that.

After dinner with his folks, Mac wandered outside, drawn automatically to his beloved miniature horses. They stood in a corner of their small paddock, huddled together against the cool of the autumn evening. At less than thirty-four inches tall they were the perfect height for petting. Their noses nuzzled him as if to say, "Welcome home."

Delighted when two of his favorite mares began poking his pockets in search of the sugar lumps he always carried, Mac moved from animal to animal, bestowing the gift on each, totally at ease here, even without his other hand. Miniatures were so gentle. They didn't prance or act up or need constant attention. They always seemed perfectly content to be exactly where they were. He envied them that.

Adele had phoned to say she was bringing the twins tomorrow. Since all eight of his miniatures were in excellent condition, Mac figured he'd saddle his two favorites and see if he could teach Francie and Franklyn to ride.

In another phone call tonight, Adele's sister Victoria had again urged his dad to instigate a trail riding program for The Haven using the Double M's horses. His father wasn't interested but Mac was, especially after a glance at the ranch books. Their income needed a boost and since their ranch hand, Gabe, had experience using horses in an equine training program for kids, trail riding seemed doable.

If he took over the ranch…

"You be nice to Francie and Franklyn when they come," Mac told his horses, veering away from making that decision, smoothing their backs as he spoke. "In the morning I'll give you a special currying so you look good."

Here among his pets, as he talked to them and smoothed their flanks, his restless soul slowly calmed and he could think more clearly. Was the Double M where he belonged? He wasn't sure, and though he tried to pray about it, God's leading seemed dulled by the guilt he felt.

"I want to do what the parents expect. I want to take over for them, give them a break, even keep their legacy going. But what if—"

And that was the problem in a nutshell. *What if?* What if he couldn't take the lifestyle? What if he messed up the ranch like he'd messed up his copilot Dave's life? And his own. What if he needed a bigger, better, faster thrill to satisfy the empty hole inside him? And what if because of Dave and that undeserved medal the military had issued him, Mac never got past the lump of guilt that lay in his gut like a ball of cement?

If he told Adele the whole truth, she'd push him to seek Dave's forgiveness, make things right with his bosses. But giving back the medal would raise too many questions and revive the crash that he only wanted to forget. His parents would be ashamed and appalled by his behavior.

Dave wouldn't be so willing to forgive the man who'd made him a paraplegic, either. Hearing his blame given voice would make the guilt ten times worse. Besides, what good would it do now? Mac had lost his hand. Dave had lost the use of his legs.

Frustrated and confused, thoughts muddled by too many questions without answers, Mac made sure the horses were safely enclosed, then walked back to the house. He was going to have to talk to Adele's aunties soon. He needed their advice to figure out his future.

The hard part would be living up to Adele's expectations.

Chapter Four

"Good old Snowball." Adele laughed the following afternoon when, after not receiving a treat, the miniature horse stamped her hoof against the ground and whinnied. "Pretty girl doesn't look much older than when I last saw her."

"She's a grandmother now." Mac's eyes softened as he patted the shaggy white horse. "Those are her children. Diver was her first. Then Flyer, both geldings. And this little one is Princess."

"She looks like a Princess. I remember when Snowball was your first and only miniature." Adele smiled as the dainty mama pushed her head against Franklyn's shoulder.

"They're like big dogs," Franklyn squealed, backing away.

"They gots different colors." Francie at least wasn't afraid of the horses. "Why?"

"Different breeds." Mac held Snowball's bridle and encouraged the children to pet her.

"But those other horses don't gots lots of colors. How come?" Francie's focus was on the corral where the Double M's full-size horses had gathered to watch them.

"I know why." Adele thought that here among his pets Mac seemed totally content and at his most charming.

"Lots of horse breeds allow only certain colors. But minis can have Appaloosa spots, pinto patches or tan buckskins with dark legs and manes and tails."

"I'm impressed you remembered." Mac grinned, then hunkered down to Francie's level. "People who own miniature horses like all the colors. Some horse shows even have competitions for the most colorful miniatures."

That grin—Adele drew in a calming breath. Why did she keep having these unusual reactions to Mac? He was just a friend, a good friend, but…

"Did your horses ever win?" a wide-eyed Franklyn wondered.

"Mac's won tons of ribbons and trophies for his minis," Adele told them proudly, then chastised herself. It wasn't as if she'd helped him win them. All she'd done was be there to cheer him on.

"Would you like to ride one of my little horses, Francie?" Mac asked after the twins had petted each one.

"Can I?" The little girl's eyes grew huge.

"I polished the saddles in case you'd want to." Mac glanced at Adele, apparently noticing, like her, that Franklyn didn't seem as enthusiastic about riding as his sister. "Would you mind waiting for your turn until after your sister has ridden?" he asked the boy.

Franklyn jerked his head in a quick nod of relief. Adele drew him with her to stand near the fence where they could listen in on Mac's quick lesson to his sister.

"This is Esther. She likes to be ridden by children, though she hasn't done it for a while." Mac led the dappled mare toward a saddle flung over the top rail. With ease he grabbed it with his one hand and set it on Esther's back, patiently explaining his actions to the curious twins as he quickly fastened the many buckles. "Okay, she's ready. Are you?"

"I guess." Francie's face scrunched up. "How do I get on?"

"I'll give you a boost and you swing your other leg over Esther's back. Put your feet in these. They're called stirrups. Ready?" At her nod he cupped his hand and encouraged her to put her foot in a stirrup and grab the saddle horn.

For Adele it was déjà vu. Mac had taught her to ride in exactly the same calm, assured way.

"Are you comfortable?" he asked.

"Uh-huh." Francie gave Adele an excited grin, then prepared for the next direction.

"Good. These are the reins. Hold them in your hand, not too tightly, and very gently press your heels against her side. That tells Esther to start walking," Mac said. "Ready? Go."

Adele noted how Mac kept his hand on the horse behind the saddle, either to calm the animal or reassure the child, or both. As Esther moved, he walked along beside her, constantly encouraging Francie. Though Adele knew he'd taught many kids to ride the larger Double M horses, as he'd taught her, she'd forgotten how gentle he was, correcting in a way that enhanced the experience for the rider. His entire focus was on Francie, anticipating her reactions and soothing her worries in an affectionate tone.

"Mac's a good teacher, isn't he?" The Double M's foreman, Gabe Webber, stood behind Adele.

"Fabulous," she murmured as Francie laughed. She didn't know Gabe well, only that he was several years older than Mac and that he'd been born and raised on a ranch but had lost it all after his father died.

"I really hope your sister pushes him to try her trail ride idea. Mac needs a new venture to test his skills and help him forget his troubles." Then Gabe tipped his hat and strode away.

What troubles? Adele didn't get the impression the foreman was talking about Mac's indecision about taking over the ranch, so what—

"Look at me, Delly!" Francie was riding by herself. Mac stood to one side, watching her intently but not interfering, though he did call out occasional directions.

Adele pulled out her phone and snapped several pictures, suddenly aware that she was including Mac in every frame. Well, why not? Francie should have memories of such a great teacher, she justified as she snapped several more. The one she liked best caught Mac midlaugh as the little girl whooped for joy.

"This one could ride the broncs, Delly," he called to her, his grin wide.

Adele caught her breath. For a moment he looked exactly like the old Mac, carefree, enjoying the moment. Then his face grew more serious as he called a halt to the ride. Francie flung her arms around Mac's neck as he helped her slide off, eyes shining with delight.

"Thank you. That was so fun!" She raced toward Adele and her brother. "You gotta try."

"I think you'll like it, Franklyn," Mac said quietly when the boy hesitated.

After some cheering words from his sister and Mac's repeated reassurances, which Adele knew were most effective because they had to do with the boy's ability to brag that he'd been horseback riding, Franklyn tentatively walked forward. Though Adele couldn't hear exactly what Mac said, as Franklyn climbed on the little horse he lost the trepidation she'd seen just moments before. Within seconds he was trotting around the paddock, calling encouragement to Esther and trying to one-up Francie.

Again Adele took a host of pictures, and again she included Mac in most of them. Then she took a final one, a close-up preserving Franklyn's disappointed expression at the end of the session and Mac's soft wistful smile. Mac and kids. He'd always adored them.

"When can I go again?" Francie's eagerness was unmistakable.

"Another day for sure," Mac said. "Want to say thank-you for the ride?"

"Horses don't know people talk," Francie asserted. Then, uncertainly, "Do they?"

"Yes." When both kids frowned at Mac, he showed them the apples he'd left in a sack outside the pen and told the children to each get one. "They understand the tone of your voice, especially when you say thank-you."

"Thank you for the ride, Esther." Francie giggled as the horse snatched the apple, gobbled it down and then bumped her head against the little girl. Esther did the same with Franklyn.

"That's how Esther says you're welcome," Mac told them with a chuckle.

Something inside Adele jumped for joy at the tender expression on his face as he brushed the horse's shaggy mane with his hand. It had been the right choice to come here with the kids. This was the real Mac, not that pretend person who wanted her to believe he was fine.

"I didn't know horses could talk." Franklyn gaped when Esther whinnied.

"Oh, they talk." Mac tossed Adele a grin. "They just don't use our words." He smoothed Franklyn's hair, or tried to. "Esther's tired now."

"Is she sick from apples?" Francie tilted her head to one side, studying the animal as if searching for a visible cause.

"No." Mac shrugged. "But she hasn't given any rides for a while. Next time you ride her she'll be a little stronger."

"Okay." Francie's eager nod made Adele smile.

"Next time I want to ride that black one," Franklyn said bravely, pointing to the adult horses. "What's his name?"

"Mr. Black. You'll need a few more lessons first, kiddo." Mac's gaze slid to Adele. "When are you coming for *your* ride?"

"Delly's too big for Esther," Francie protested.

"I am, but you both did very well," Adele praised, pleased that both the children and Mac seemed exhilarated by the adventure. "I'll come for a ride soon," she promised Mac. They left the paddock but stood outside watching as all the minis gathered by the fence. "They're expecting something."

"Yep. Carrots." Mac retrieved a bunch from the nearby tack room. "One to each horse, okay? Share."

Franklyn and Francie carefully meted out the treat while Adele and Mac watched.

"You looked worried for a minute there, Mama," Mac teased as he searched her face. "Don't you trust me?"

"Of course. I've always trusted you, Mac." *Except when you're pretending.* She ignored his narrowed gaze and the quiver of unease it brought her. "I *was* a little tense."

"Because?"

"I want to build a life with the twins. To do that, it's important that they fit in here, enjoy the same things I do. I should have known they'd love it." She grinned. "How many kids have you taught to ride?"

"Enough." But Mac didn't smile. Instead his forehead pleated in a frown. "You're certain adopting is what you want, Delly?"

"Couldn't be surer," she said cheerily, ignoring the flutter of apprehension she couldn't quite quench. "I *am* going to have my perfect family, Mac."

"Perfect?" He frowned. "What family is perfect? Life's

uncertain. Anything could happen. I don't want you to be disappointed if…"

"No. Don't say it," Adele said loudly enough that Francie and Franklyn turned to frown at her. She dropped her voice. "*This* is why God led me back. To help with The Haven *and* to be a mom."

"You know I only want the best for you, Delly." His arm slid around her shoulders, hugging her to his side.

"I know, and I appreciate your concern." She hugged him back, missing the contact when he suddenly released her. "I wish—"

"What?" Mac frowned then nodded. "Gina."

"Yes. Why can't I find her, Mac?" She bit her lip before glancing sideways at him. "How can my family be perfect without my sister?"

He studied her for several long moments before his eyes lightened and a comical smile curved his lips.

"As your aunts would say, 'Trust in the Lord with all thine heart; and lean not unto thine own understanding,'" Mac recited.

"'In all thy ways acknowledge him, and he shall direct thy paths,'" Adele finished the verse with a sigh. "I know that. I should—I've heard it enough times. But sometimes it's hard not to get frustrated. It's been so long since I've seen Gina." She couldn't help the catch in her voice or the familiar welling of loss that despite years of Tillie and Margaret's loving had never really left. "I miss her."

"Hang in there, Delly. You'll find her." Mac's warm fingers closed around hers for a second, then dropped away as his mother called to them from the ranch house, offering coffee or cocoa and cookies served on the sunny deck. After one last pet to the horses Francie and Franklyn hurried toward the house while Adele and Mac followed at a slower pace.

"After seeing the twins on your minis I'm more certain than ever that they and I belong together." Her confidence returned at the sound of the twins' carefree laughter.

Adele wondered if Mac understood how much she envied what he'd had. He'd grown up safe and secure on the ranch. His parents didn't fight, smash things or beat him. The police didn't settle arguments at the Double M. Nobody had ever taken Mac away.

Of course, after Adele arrived at The Haven she, too, had grown up in a wonderful home filled with love. She'd had an amazing youth; the aunties had loved her as much as anyone could. She was going, God willing, to be the twins' mom.

Yet a part of her still speculated about love, about that perfect someone to whom she meant more than anyone else in the world. Then reality slapped her in the face, reminding her that both her parents had remarried several times and neither of them had found a lasting relationship. She'd tried with Jeff and Rafe, but it had been a case of like parents, like daughter.

Adele preceded Mac onto the deck, smiling as the kids oohed and aahed over six new puppies.

"Easy with those babies, you two, or their mama won't like it." Mac nodded his approval when the twins immediately grew gentler in petting the tiny chocolate Labs that spilled off a comfy cushion on the deck where their mother lay watching them.

"We're here, Mom," Mac called. He held Adele's chair before sitting across from her.

His gaze was so intense she shifted uncomfortably, relieved when Eva McDowell appeared with a big tray. Mac took it from her so she could hug Adele. Once introduced, the twins also received a hug before being shown how to wash their hands under the outside faucet. They returned to the deck, damp and giggling.

"It's good to have you home, dear." Eva's smile could melt icicles, just like her son's. "Eat up. There's lots for everyone." She hurried toward the door, pausing to add, "If you need me, just call."

"Thank you. New quilting project on the go?" Adele asked with a wink at Mac.

"Yes. Tillie loaned me the pattern and it's a beauty." She fluttered one hand. "See you later."

Adele took a sip of coffee without thinking, then grimaced. "Oh, boy."

"You should know better," Mac scolded. He dumped the contents of their mugs over the railing then filled both with cocoa from the carafe. "I think that's safe. And the cookies are your own coconut oatmeal recipe. They should be edible." He bit into one as if to test, then nodded. "Good. What's the next step in finding Gina?"

"I don't know." Adele cupped the mug in her hand and peered across the paddock to the valley beyond. Trees clad in vibrant oranges, glimmering golds and rosy reds shone below craggy tips barely dusted with snow. The warm sun on her back felt like hope.

"A guy I know took up private investigation when he left the military. I could email him, ask what you should try," Mac offered.

"That would be great." Adele munched on a cookie thoughtfully. "What about you? What's your next step?"

"I'm going to tell the parents to go on their cruise." He shrugged at her surprise. "Why not? Gabe agrees that we can keep the place going while they take a break."

"Fantastic." Adele frowned. "Is your dad okay to travel?"

"That's what I asked Doc Perry yesterday. He said that

minus the stress of the ranch, Dad should do well with a change." Mac peered into the distance. "They haven't been away in years."

"Are you considering Victoria's trail ride idea?" she dared ask.

"Maybe." Mac arched an eyebrow at her grin. "It might not work for me, Delly. I'll have to try it once or twice to see how it goes."

Mac was staying. Adele's heart felt light and carefree. *Why did that matter so much?*

"When are *we* going for a ride together?" Mac demanded.

"As soon as you ask me." Funny how she couldn't stop smiling. "Tonight?"

"Tonight? Mom and Dad are having the pastor for dinner. Can I let you know?" Slightly distracted by Adele's swift response to his invitation, Mac turned his attention to the children just in time to see them sneak bits of cookie. "Don't even think about feeding those puppies," he warned. "Chocolate will make them sick."

"Oh. C'n we get a puppy, Delly?" Francie asked with a full mouth.

"We already have Spot and Dot at The Haven," Adele reminded. "Springer spaniels my aunts rescued," she explained to him.

Mac nodded. "Springers are good pets."

"I don't think my aunties want more dogs," Adele explained to Francie in a cautious tone. Mac figured it was because she knew that if Francie wheedled hard enough, the softhearted aunts would quickly give in.

"You can come and visit the puppies here," he offered. It would be fun to have kids on the ranch again.

"'Kay," Franklyn agreed with a firm nod. "When we visit the minis."

"When will that be?" Mac asked Adele.

"I'm not sure. There's a big group of kids arriving tomorrow for the weekend, with counselors, so I'm going to be busy."

"How busy can you be? You've been prepping stuff for days. The twins told me," he admitted when she arched one eyebrow at him. He knew nothing about cooking, but he wanted to spend more time with Adele, to catch up on their friendship. He glanced into the house before whispering, "What's on the menu tomorrow night?"

"Chuckwagon chili on a bun." She frowned. "Why are we whispering?"

"Tomorrow night is Mom's Tofu Tumble night."

"Oh." Adele's smile emphasized the dimples in her cheeks, which in turn emphasized her wholesome loveliness. "What's that?"

"Lentils and sprouts and a bunch of other stuff I can't identify wrapped in some kind of brown-veined leaf. Tastes worse than liver." Mac pretended to gag. He could keep carrying on for ages just to hear her wonderful laugh.

"Liver and onions. Delicious." Adele giggled when he grabbed his stomach in pretend pain. The twins stared at them.

"Don't make me eat it. Please, have pity. Invite me over for dinner, I beg you." Since he wasn't sure his tactics were working, he changed strategies. "If you don't, you'll be sorry when you come to see me in intensive care and the nurse tells you that if only someone had prevented me from partaking of that—"

"Stop it, con artist." Delly shook her head in reprimand, though her amber eyes still crinkled at the corners. "Your mother is a good cook. A bit adventurous, but that's not a bad thing."

"Yeah? Want some more coffee?" Mac shot back, grinning when she wrinkled her nose and shook her head. "She says everything she makes is heart-healthy, but Dad looks even paler now than when I first came home, especially when she calls him for dinner."

"You're a terrible tease, Mac," she reproved.

"Not teasing." He sighed. "He looked awful this morning but insisted on riding up to the north quarter alone to check a fence because Gabe's tied up today." He frowned. "They have to get out of here and on that cruise."

"Then you can decide whether or not you're staying permanently."

Mac didn't respond. Adele gave him a questioning look before she rose and asked the children to help carry their dishes inside to the sink. That done, she called her thanks to Mac's mother, who remained in her quilting room in the basement but invited them back to the ranch anytime. Then Mac walked her to her car.

"You fasten Francie in, I'll help Franklyn," she said.

He complied, encouraging Francie's giggles and Franklyn's outright laughter at his knock-knock jokes.

"You're nothing but a big kid yourself, Mac McDowell." Adele fastened her seat belt and started the car.

"I know. It's always been a problem." Still acting the clown, Mac thrust his head inside the car window. "That's why I should come to dinner with the other kids," he said, blinking rapidly in comic enticement. "Right?"

"You're always welcome, Mac." Adele shook her head at his smug smile. "Say thank-you for the ride, children."

Amid the kids' loud calls of thank-you, she drove out of the yard and under the wrought-iron arches with the Double M script.

Mac's world suddenly lost its brilliance. With a sigh he headed for the tack room. Time to saddle a horse and check out his dad.

Work was supposed to be a panacea, right? That thought didn't help lighten his mood.

But there was dinner with Adele at The Haven to look forward to.

"Mac's nice, isn't he?" Francie said as they drove toward home. "On'y sometimes he gets sad. How come, Delly?"

She was about to respond when Franklyn chimed in.

"Aunt Tillie said it's 'cause of his accident. She said he got hurted real bad and not just his body." Franklyn frowned. "What else can you get hurted, Delly?"

"Your heart, honey. Like it hurts inside. Understand?" She glanced in the rearview mirror and saw them nodding. "Maybe Aunt Tillie means Mac's heart hurts."

She tucked in a CD and let the kids sing along while she pondered that thought. Hearts usually got hurt because someone else was involved.

Who had been involved with Mac and why did it make his heart hurt?

Though Adele asked herself that question all the way home, she couldn't come up with a suitable answer as to what, other than his accident, had changed her friend Mac. But she was going to find out.

Chapter Five

"Are you mad, Delly?"

"No. I was just trying to make your social worker understand—why do you ask that, Francie?" Adele set down her cell phone and frowned at the little girl.

"You sounded mad when you were talking on the phone."

"Watch it, Delly. Little pitchers," Mac said sotto voce.

"Huh?" Francie shrugged when no one explained. "He said we c'n ride the big horses."

"Sometime. *With me*," Mac emphasized as he stretched his long legs under The Haven's kitchen table.

"Are you sure?" Adele didn't want to underestimate him but reining in a horse while controlling a wiggly child seemed a bit—much.

"You mean for a guy who's only recently returned to the saddle, or for a guy who only has one arm?" Mac's face tightened. "You doubt me, Adele?"

"No, but—"

"I've been riding for a couple of hours every day since the day after I came home." He looked angry. "I'm competent. I have to be, with Mom and Dad leaving."

"When's that?" she asked to change the subject.

"Tomorrow." Mac was not to be diverted. "The twins will be safe with me, Delly. You can trust me. Was that why you canceled our ride last night?"

"It was 'cause of me. I din't feel good." Franklyn rubbed his stomach. "I don't feel good now."

"I'm sure you'll be fine, honey," Adele assured him with a meaningful glance at Mac. "Now you two go change into your jeans while I talk to Mac."

"'Kay." Francie scooted out of the room. Franklyn followed at a much slower pace.

"He doesn't want to ride with me?" Mac guessed.

"He's a bit nervous but I think he'll be okay once he's actually on the horse." She studied him, noting how much more relaxed he'd looked than the day she'd first seen him. "What about the trail rides, Mac?"

"I'm still thinking about it." He sipped the coffee she'd poured for him, eyes averted.

"What's to think about?" she pressed.

"Liability. If a kid got hurt or—"

"Victoria checked into that. We're fully covered," she rushed to assure him.

"We're not. And liability insurance is expensive. The Double M hasn't been doing that well the last couple of years. I'm not sure we can take on another big bill." Mac still didn't look at her. That was how she knew he was worried about more than insurance.

"Tell the truth, Mac. Are you concerned you might not be able to handle a trail ride?" She sat down across from him, wishing now that she hadn't said anything about his ability to take the twins for a ride.

"Yes. Before, if a kid floundered or a horse stumbled, I'd reach out and grab the reins. Take control." He lifted his head, his blue-green eyes shadowed. "If that happened now, there's nothing I could do. The first rule of horsemanship is to retain control of your *own* animal. I can do that just fine, even with one of the twins aboard. But I don't have a hand to spare." He looked at the one he had as if it offended him. "I'd like to do the trail riding, Delly, if only because it would be something new and different and interesting. I'm just not sure I can."

The twins returned but Adele wanted a few more minutes alone with Mac, so she asked them to walk the dogs on the little path around the house. When they were gone she studied the big cowboy, her heart aching for the loss, not only of his arm, but of his self-assurance.

But she stifled her sympathy, knowing Mac would hate that.

"There must be other ways you could compensate?"

"Some." She could tell he didn't like facing his weakness. "Try to corral the animal with my horse, that kind of thing. But I've never done it with my hand and half my arm gone and I don't want to practice on foster kids who've never ridden."

"Then you can practice on me." She rose and checked the roast in the oven. Then she picked up the phone. "Stella, are you free to give me a hand this afternoon? Good. Here's what I need." She laid out the details to the woman who'd been assisting her in the kitchen for the past two days, answered her questions, thanked her and then hung up.

"Adele, you don't have to do this," Mac said, frowning. "The idea of me taking the kids this afternoon was to free you up."

"I am freed up. Stella's coming. And I've decided to go riding today." She gave him a severe look. "I am going to be your guinea pig, but so help me, Mac, if you let me get thrown—"

His burst of laughter made her smile. Much better when Mac was laughing.

Twenty minutes later they were at the Double M, where Mac was giving Francie a ride on his horse, Nightshade, a big black stallion. Adele had questioned him about that choice, but Mac was clearly going for broke. If he couldn't manage his favorite horse with the twins and later, on a trail with her, she knew he wouldn't agree to give the rides.

After Franklyn had his turn, Gabe took the twins to see the puppies, leaving Adele with a brown mare she'd never ridden before.

"Her name is Pesky." Mac's face wore an odd look.

"What kind of name is that?" She climbed on with trepidation. "Where's Star? I know her."

"That's exactly the reason I asked Gabe to saddle Pesky. Star is familiar with your riding and probably wouldn't react the same as would a horse with a new rider. Your group would be totally new to our horses," he explained. "I want the unexpected, so I can prepare."

"But—" Seeing the implacable glint in his meltwater eyes, Adele gave up. "Okay, but just remember what I said about me falling off," she warned.

"Do that stiff pride of yours good, Delly," Mac teased. Then he got serious. "As much as possible give Pesky her head. We're trying to emulate untried riders, remember?"

She nodded nervously, aware that her horse was now heading for the rails. Before she could react and rein in Pesky, Mac had ridden between them and was using Nightshade to nudge her away.

"Let's see how she'll follow." Mac leaned over, undid the gate and rode his horse through. Pesky followed, then suddenly veered right. "Don't rein her in," he called as he refastened the gate.

Somehow, he managed to arrive at Adele's side just before Pesky entered a grove of trees. Mac swiftly moved in front. For a few minutes Pesky seemed content to follow

Nightshade, until a rabbit raced across the trail. Immediately she lengthened her stride and took off, on a mission to chase that rabbit. Adele tugged on the reins but could not control the disobedient animal. Overhanging branches slapped at her face, and to top it off, a light rain began to fall. Ahead lay the banks of a stream. Heart in her throat, she wondered if she could hang on if Pesky tried to jump it.

She should have known better. Mac raced past to block the way. Now, with dense brush closing in on either side, there was nowhere for Pesky to go. She stopped short, almost throwing Adele.

"Are you okay?" Mac held Pesky's bridle while he inspected Adele's scraped face. He winced. "I'm sorry, Delly. I didn't think she'd go off like that."

Furious, she gritted her teeth and snapped, "I would not put this horse on any trail ride anywhere at any time." She brushed her gloved fingers against her stinging cheek. "She's useless. Why do you keep her?"

"Ah, Delly, you always demand perfection." Mac sounded amused.

She glared at him, unappeased.

"Pesky isn't useless, and we don't keep her because she's perfect. We keep her because she's an amazing mother to some of the strongest colts the Double M has ever had. That more than makes up for her lack of riding suitability." Mac petted the horse's neck, murmuring soothing things.

"Oh." Adele studied the animal with new perspective.

"But that little incident adds to my worry," he added with a frown. "If one horse bolts as she just did, and another follows, we'll have problems."

"Which is why Gabe would be there." Adele adjusted her tired old Stetson to keep the rain out of her eyes. "Anyway, I'm guessing you'd set apart time at the beginning for the kids to get familiar with their horses before they actually ride, right?" She waited for his nod. "So that would give you a chance to assess if an animal or kid was going to be a problem."

"True." He watched her, eyes narrowed as she arched her back. "Sore?"

"Wet," she corrected. "Let's finish this. What next?"

"See if she'll follow my lead." Mac waited for her nod of consent, then began walking Nightshade. He turned several times to observe how her mare followed. After a few minutes he stopped and urged her to precede him.

"Where to?" Adele asked.

"Our spot." Mac simply looked at her without offering another hint. He didn't need to. Adele knew exactly where he meant. She just wasn't sure if she could find it anymore.

"That was ages ago. I'm not sure—"

"Some things you never forget," he encouraged quietly. "Besides, I want to see if she'll obey or if something will pop up and draw her off the trail again, and if I can handle it."

"You're the boss." After a quick glance around to get her bearings, Adele directed the horse left at the first fork in the path.

During their ascent to the lookout point, Adele kept her hands loose on the reins, letting Pesky have her head. The horse plodded along as if she knew the exact spot Mac meant. This time she evidenced no distraction when a mother deer and her two fawns appeared.

Ten minutes later Adele pulled to a stop. That same rush of delight at being home filled her as she glanced around. Their lovely private glade at the crest of the hill looked unchanged.

"See? You found it." Mac slid off Nightshade, threw his reins over a branch, then offered a hand to help her down. He fastened Pesky more securely, then fed both horses a carrot. "I knew you wouldn't forget our spot. How many times did we come here?"

"Hundreds. For every celebration. After you won that first bronc riding competition. And the second, third, fourth…" Adele walked forward to stand under the shelter of a massive spruce tree and stared down across the now-golden meadow, allowing those happy memories to flicker through her mind. "When you took the championship for this area. And when you won a tryout on the mountain climbing team."

"When you won that bursary at graduation. And after you got accepted to cooking school," Mac reminded.

Choosing a massive boulder they'd often shared, Adele sat on a corner, where she was mostly sheltered from the gentle rain. She tilted her head and studied Mac.

"Why didn't you ever pursue the climbing thing?"

"Didn't think it was an option." He sat beside her, his face thoughtful. "After Carter died, I figured it was up to me to take his place on the Double M."

"But you quit college," she pointed out, admiring his handsome profile as he studied the land around him. "Duty didn't matter then?"

Mac snorted.

"More a case of being overcome by the flying bug." He shifted to look at her. "Truth is, Delly, it wasn't until I was on the base that I really thought about the Double M and my parents and what I'd done. By then it was too late. I was committed."

"Maybe that's why you did it," she offered quietly. His quizzical look made her shrug. "Maybe you were unconsciously searching for an escape route and maybe that day the air show offered it."

He thought about it, nose wrinkling. "Maybe." But his tone expressed his doubt.

"So what's the verdict? Will you do the trail rides?" she prodded, knowing her sister would want a firm no from him before she approached other ranchers. "Did today help?"

"Sort of." Mac glanced over one shoulder at the grazing horses. "Pesky is the worst of our herd for getting side-tracked. Once she forgot about that rabbit, she was okay, but still, I wouldn't use her."

"Good idea. In my humble opinion, being great at motherhood doesn't outweigh her shortcomings." Adele kept pressing him because she sensed that Mac needed to do this, if only to prove to himself that he could. "Then that's a yes to the trail rides?"

"Pushy or what?" Exasperated, he nodded. "I'll take one group as a test. If there are no major issues with that, I'll consider taking another. I don't want to sign up for several months, though."

"Why not?" Adele frowned. "You want to leave yourself an out in case you get bored with it?" When Mac shook his head she chided, "Tell the truth."

"You and your demand for truth." Mac rolled his eyes. "I *am* telling the truth. It's not an out. It's the idea of setting up a program without having any goals. What's the point of these trail rides?"

"Having fun, maybe?" she suggested.

"These kids could have fun in other ways besides riding. What difference would I make to their world?"

His comment surprised Adele. Carefree, playful Mac wanted to make a difference in a foster kid's world? But then she remembered how he'd made a world of difference to her. Maybe she was only now seeing him as a man, without the veil of admiration she'd worn when they were kids.

"You'll teach them new skills. They'll be doing something different," she mused.

"Coming to The Haven isn't different enough?" Mac frowned. "What do they leave with? A couple of rides in the forest?"

"What's wrong with that?" she demanded.

"If a little ride is all they need we could hook the horses in a circle and they could sit on them and go around and around. Like a carnival." There was an edge of frustration in his words.

"I get your point." Adele reconsidered. "A lesson and a short ride is probably all there's time for with weekend riders. But for the repeaters—kids who return, or for those who come for longer, maybe you could hold a little event before they leave, so they could demonstrate their new skills." Immediately Adele noticed Mac's body shift as his interest grew.

"Define this event." His eyes now sparkled, the blank stare gone.

"I don't know. A kind of beginner rodeo? That's your area." She frowned when he kept staring at her, waiting. "Moving from a walk to a trot or a canter? Sidestepping? Your horses already know all those things, so it would simply be a matter of teaching the kids."

A long silence stretched. Adele found it odd that she couldn't read Mac's thoughts as easily as she once had. Time and distance had certainly made a difference between them.

"It could work," he said finally. "We've got a building—"

"Where you used to train for the rodeos. I remember." Excited, she clasped her hands together. "It would be perfect, especially when the weather gets cooler and messier."

"Originally Dad used it for breaking colts, and later I used it to train for the rodeos. It works for an arena, but we'd need some seating for observers," he said, thinking it through out loud.

"Simple benches. Nothing fancy. It's a ranch." That meant he was going to do it, that he'd be staying? Adele's excitement grew as Mac listed things he needed to do.

"A lot of work would have to be done before it snows," he said a few moments later.

"Why? Snow never bothered our riding," she said.

"These kids are newcomers," he reminded. "Some are young. If something happened and one got separated from the group, there should be markers for them to follow and find their way back."

"A fence?" Dubious about installing that with the ground already freezing up, never mind the cost of acres of fencing, Adele frowned.

"More like bright, unmistakable flags to mark the way or little posted signs. It might work." Mac fell silent, lost in thought.

Adele patiently waited, shifting uncomfortably as a chill set in. When an icy raindrop tumbled off her hat and onto her nose, she shivered.

"Mac, let's go get the twins and have hot cocoa at The Haven," she said finally.

"Why The Haven? Our place is—"

"Very busy with your parents packing for their trip. Let's go to The Haven, if Gabe hasn't already taken Francie and Franklyn back," she added.

"Gabe loves kids. He'll have kept them busy," Mac assured her. "And probably worn them out."

"Not likely. Those two don't wear out." She checked her watch and gasped. "I had no idea we'd been gone so long." In her rush to leave she moved too quickly and stumbled on a tree root, falling face-first onto the wet forest floor. "Oof!"

"Are you okay?" Mac's hand under her elbow helped her stand. He tried to brush off the pine needles and assorted detritus that clung to her clothes, but it was pointless. "Now you're really wet," he muttered.

"And filthy." Adele grimaced at her dirty clothing before another shiver took over. "Forget it. Let's go." She swung up into her saddle, fingers tightening on the reins as Pesky tried to edge away. "Oh, no, you don't. I've got your number now, lady. On the trail and no deviations."

Pesky lifted her head, gave a snort of disapproval but moved sedately over the same path they'd followed here. Mac hooted with laughter.

"What's so funny?" she demanded, glancing around.

Of course, Pesky chose that precise moment to take off after a grouse. Almost unseated, Adele fought for control, grateful when she saw Mac's gloved fingers close over Pesky's bridle, slowing her to a controllable gait. His own reins were looped over the stub of his missing arm.

"I knew she'd try something. She didn't like standing still for so long." The slash of white from his grin made her stomach dip with attraction. What was that about?

"You might have warned me," she muttered, disgusted when he lifted his hand and wiped a smear of mud from her cheek. "This ride proves at least one thing."

"Let me guess." Mac leaned back in his saddle, obviously trying not to laugh. "You'll never ride Pesky again?"

"Okay, two things," she snarled as she again turned the horse in the correct direction. "One, I am never riding this animal again. Two, you just managed that unforeseen problem very well. I doubt you have anything to worry about with trail rides."

"Maybe." Mac said nothing more as he led the way back to the barn.

Once inside they removed the tackle and wiped the animals down before putting them in their stalls. When

Mac handed her a small bucket of oats for Pesky, Adele glared at him.

"You think she deserves this?" His quickly smothered chortle of laughter did nothing to enhance her dark mood.

"You're bac— Delly!" Francie gaped at her. "Did you falled off?"

"No, I tripped. I'm soaking wet and I want to go home. Go get in the car," she told the two children. "On the way home you can tell me what you've been doing. Thank you, Gabe," she added, smiling at the tall man standing behind them. "I never expected to be gone so long." She frowned at the splatter on his jacket but couldn't discern what it was. "Are you okay?"

"I'll survive," he growled. That became a full-fledged smile as the twins thanked him.

"It was so fun. I never seed a bull before," Franklyn said.

"A bull?" One glance from the kids to Gabe's pursed lips to Mac's pretend-blank stare told Adele that neither man intended to explain. "Into the car, children. *You* can tell me all about the bull on the way home." She dumped half the bucket of oats into Pesky's feeder, then poured the rest back into the feed sack. "Don't you dare give her anymore," she warned the men. "She doesn't deserve it."

Adele stomped toward the door. She'd almost made it when Mac called out.

"I think I'll take a rain check on that cocoa, Delly. Thanks anyway. See you later." Mirth underlay the words, but wet, cold and frustrated, Adele didn't even turn to glance at him.

Mac was going to do the trail rides. That was enough, for now.

"Will I sound like a wuss if I say I'm glad you're here to help with the Double M's first trail ride?" Mac wasn't quite sure of Adele's mood after yesterday, so her sunny smile was a relief. And there was nothing to show she'd bit the dust—er, mud, twenty-four hours ago.

"As if a big, strong cowboy like you could ever look like a wimp," she teased. "Your parents got to their plane all right?"

"They texted me after they'd boarded. They're pretty excited." He wasn't going to admit that his anticipation was mixed with worry about running their spread for the next few months. "It was nice of Ben to drive them in."

"Vic's husband is a good guy. He had some stuff to do in Edmonton. He said it was no trouble." Adele patted the dun-colored mare nearest her as her foster sister arrived at the Double M with a van load of six kids. "There's Victoria, so here we go."

"Yeah." Mac exhaled and offered a silent prayer that he wouldn't mess this up. After all his indecision, he really wanted these trail rides to take off and not only because The Haven was being very generous with their payment for the program. Some kid part of him desperately wanted to show Delly and himself that he could do this, that he wasn't less of a man now that he'd lost his hand.

As Mac introduced Gabe and the horses, he mentally assessed each guest. A few minutes later and after a short conference, he found Gabe's assessment jibed with his on which child should go with which horse. Then Gabe took over, demonstrating the way to curry their mounts, which they'd decided was a good way to help the kids feel more at ease with the animals. Victoria stood back, constantly evaluating her guests' responses to their program and making occasional notes.

"So far, so good," Adele murmured.

"Yep. Where are the twins today?" The words slipped out, surprising Mac with his need to know about the two mischief makers. He enjoyed it when they were around. But did Delly, he wondered as he noted the lines around her eyes. Was coming to the Double M, arranging meals at The Haven, *and* taking care of Francie and Franklyn too much?

"It's the twins' first day at preschool. Shelley Paraday agreed to let them attend even though they came to her program late. I hope they enjoy it." Adele chewed her bottom lip. "I wasn't going to leave, but Shelley said they'd settle in better without me. I hope she's right."

"They'll be fine, Mama." He patted her shoulder awkwardly, wishing he had more to offer than that. A moment later he caught Gabe's glance and stepped forward. His turn. "Now we're going to talk about saddling your horse," he told the group of kids.

Once Mac had gone through the routines, he, Adele and Gabe each took two of the guests and worked with them to saddle up, fastening cinches and ensuring the riders would be safe. Every so often Mac felt Adele's stare. He'd glance at her and her grin would spread, eyes twinkling as she made a circle with her thumb and forefinger in an "OK" sign. What a cheerleader.

Finally, assured the group was ready, Mac called out, "Mount up."

It took a while but eventually everyone was seated on their horse. Mac asked Adele to demonstrate use of the reins, ignoring her frown before she trotted her horse in front and, with exaggerated motions, showed how to control the horse.

"Our horses are used to being ridden so they will respond to slight pressure of the reins. You don't have to tug or yank," he explained. "That hurts their mouths and they don't like it."

Again he, Adele and Gabe each took two students, and

far quicker than Mac had expected, the preteens mastered coaxing their horses to walk in a circle. He rode from one to the next, correcting posture, knee placement and control.

"Not bad, huh?" Adele cantered over to him, obviously pleased. "They learn fast."

"Faster than I anticipated. I hadn't planned this but there's plenty of time left in their lesson. Let's see if we can teach them to trot."

An hour later, elated by what they'd accomplished, Mac watched as the kids, laughing and happy, waved goodbye.

"Success, I'd say." Victoria turned from counting as the last child boarded to grin at Mac.

"I've got a few things I'll change, but all in all it's a great start." Adele's smug smile made him laugh. "Yes, you were right, Delly. They'll be back tomorrow?" he asked Victoria, who waited to drive the kids back to The Haven.

"Nine a.m.?" she suggested. "How about we try a little longer, like maybe a couple of hours to ride a ways into the forest?"

Mac nodded, and with a wave of her hand Victoria drove away.

"I've got to go, too. It's almost lunchtime. Stella is good, but I still need to be there." Adele shoved her riding gloves into her back pocket. She took a step toward her car, paused and turned back. "Are you joining us for lunch, Mac? Cream-of-potato soup and roast beef sandwiches."

He knew she knew it was his favorite.

"I'd love that, but I'll be a bit late. Gabe and I need to review." He loved the way her blond hair shone under the black Stetson. "Is that okay?"

"Sure." She shrugged. "Take all the time you need. Bring Gabe. I might even give you the hot cocoa I promised yesterday." Smirking, with not a hair out of place,

Adele drove away as the first of the season's soft snow-flakes drifted down from a now-leaden sky.

Mac had tons to do. There was tomorrow's trail ride to plan, fences to mend in the south pasture, a coyote who'd been stalking their prize Angus cattle to find, the minis to feed and a host of other responsibilities. But after he'd spoken to Gabe, he ignored the chiding voice in the recesses of his mind that reminded him of his duty. Instead he climbed into his truck and drove to The Haven. As he thrust the gearshift into Park, he sat for a moment, surveying the massive stone house with its lush forested background.

"Okay, God. I guess I'm part of this ministry now and it feels good." He stared at his empty sleeve, a warm feeling settling inside. "At least I don't feel quite as useless as I did when I first lost my hand. Are You telling me I might have something to offer these kids?"

No audible response, of course. But some inner voice reminded him that if he stayed at the Double M, he'd have many chances to spend time with the twins. And Delly. It was almost as if he was back where he belonged.

Except for Dave and that stupid medal I don't deserve.

A rap on the truck window startled him.

"Are you expecting car service?" Adele grinned at him. "Not gonna happen. Gabe?"

"Said his lunch was a stew in his slow cooker. But he thanked you." Mac got out and walked beside her as she hurried toward the house. "What were you doing outside?"

"Calling the dogs. They've been terrorizing a squirrel." She closed the kitchen door behind him. "The starving masses left you only one bowl of soup, but you can have three sandwiches. Mustard?"

Because he knew she knew the answer to that, Mac cocked an eyebrow up as if to ask, *Really?*

"Some things never change." Adele chuckled as she

added a generous dollop of mustard to each sandwich. "I've already eaten," she explained. "But I'll sit with you and have a cup of tea with my cake."

"Mmm." Mac savored the creamy soup with just a hint of dill before asking, "What kind of cake?"

"Carrot, banana or chocolate. Take your pick."

"Carrot, banana *and* chocolate." Mac grinned when she rolled her eyes. Man, he loved being back here, with her, just like in the old days.

"Mac?"

"Yeah." Adele's bent head and sloped shoulders weren't those of the confident girl he'd chummed with. "What's wrong?"

She held out a letter as tears streamed down her cheeks. "Look."

Mac scanned it, noting the official government logo at the top. *We are unable to provide the current address of Gina Parker...*

"Ah, Delly." He set down his soup spoon and slid his arm around her, hugging her for a moment to share her sadness. "I'm so sorry."

"I know." She sniffed, dashed away her tears and forced a smile. "I'm just being silly, expecting they'd know where she is after all this time. At least I finally got an answer."

"Right. So now you can move on." Mac was a bit relieved when she rose to get another tissue. Hugging Adele now wasn't like it had been when they were kids. It was— different, though he couldn't have explained exactly why that should be.

"I don't suppose you've heard anything from your friend?" she said as she returned to sit at the table. "The one who might have an idea how to help?"

"He texted. He's tied up with a family emergency at the moment, but said he'd get back to me with some suggestions as soon as he can." Mac felt bad as disappointment filled her face. "His mom's dying, so I don't know how long that will be. I'm sorry."

"It's okay. I guess it's just another roadblock that's supposed to teach me patience." Adele glared at him. "Don't you dare remind me patience isn't my strong suit."

Mac made a motion of zipping his lips, then continued eating his lunch.

"What about you?" she asked when he finally leaned back to savor his mug of cocoa.

"What about me?"

"Mac McDowell, you know very well what I'm asking. Are you okay after today?" Her severe look and tone of voice reminded him of his third-grade teacher, and that made him snicker.

"I'm fine, thanks, Delly. Tomorrow might be a little more difficult, but I'll be fine then, too. I'm always fine," he reminded her, thinking how far that was from the truth.

"Are you?" Her amber eyes continued their relentless search. "I get this feeling that there's something you're not telling me. Is—is something wrong? Because you know, Mac, whatever it is, I will understand."

"Something like what?" He couldn't hold her gaze. He had to look away.

"You tell me."

"Nothing to tell." He plunked his empty cocoa mug on the table and stood. "That was a fantastic lunch. Thank you. But I gotta go. I promised Gabe I'd help him with chores this afternoon."

He'd just grabbed his Stetson when she asked, "If something *was* wrong, you'd tell me, wouldn't you, Mac? You wouldn't keep me in the dark?"

"Hey!" He whirled around and stared at her. "I'm fine. I just need time to adjust to losing my hand, that's all."

"That's all." Her disgust was obvious as she smacked the cups into the dishwasher. "As if all that happened was that a little leech fell on your arm and someone had to pry it off." She glared at him, bright spots of color on her porcelain cheeks. "Stop pretending, Mac. If you won't tell me the truth, don't say anything."

"Adele." Heaving a silent sigh of frustration, Mac walked to her and pushed her chin up so that she had to look at him. "I'm fine. Everything is an adjustment for me, including being back on the ranch. But I'm managing, especially with you providing such amazing food."

Her eyes glittered like hard topaz chips and he knew he had to do better than mere flattery.

"Give me some time to adjust, Delly. If things aren't exactly the way they were between us, it doesn't mean something's wrong," he chided gently, feeling like a liar. "Everybody changes. Look at you, becoming a mom. It's been a long time since I was here and now I'm in charge of the entire ranch. It's a bit daunting. I'll be fine—soon."

Mac felt like a jerk for playing on her sympathy like this, but the last thing he wanted was Adele's constant questions or pressing him about his past. She, with her big, generous heart, wouldn't understand his actions and that would put their friendship at risk.

Right now, Mac couldn't contemplate his world without Adele there to encourage and support him.

"I'm sorry, pal." She hugged him tightly, then suddenly let him go. Some silly part of him wished that embrace hadn't ended. "I know it can't be easy for you. I guess I'm reading things into what's happened. It's just that I want things to be perfect between us, like they were before."

"They weren't always perfect," he reminded quietly. "Anyway, we can't go back. We're not kids anymore."

"I know." Adele shook her head in self-reproof. "Go, do

your work. Come back for supper. The twins would love to see you and we can talk some more."

"Thanks. We'll see how work goes." Mac left as quickly as he could, his guilt growing.

As he struggled through the afternoon's sloppy wet snow, as he herded cattle, prepared a new course for The Haven's riders tomorrow and fed his miniatures, he kept imagining Adele's voice, visualizing her face, feeling her disgust if she ever found out that he'd caused the accident that injured his friend.

Mac didn't return to The Haven for supper, didn't visit the twins, though he sorely missed their cheery smiles. Instead he opened a can of beans and heated it. He ate, fed the mother dog who now resided in front of the fireplace with her puppies, straightened up the house and started a load of laundry.

But his mind was with Adele and the twins, going through their story-time ritual, picturing Francie's endless questions before toothbrushing and bedtime kisses took over. Kids had always been part of his imagined future.

He was never going to be a father. The fact suddenly hit home like blunt-force trauma.

"What is my future, God?" he cried out. "You said You had plans for me, to prosper me and not to harm me. What are those plans?"

Mac hated the empty silence. He turned on the television hoping to cut off his melancholy thoughts. It didn't help so he shut it off. His gaze strayed to the shiny medal sitting proudly on the mantel, mocking him.

Meritorious Service Cross. As if his actions merited anything but shame. He'd messed up so badly someone else got hurt. Sure, his hunch had been proven right when the crash had revealed a flaw in the engine that could have proven catastrophic to troops in the field. But now Mac figured they'd have found it eventually. Anyway, he sure didn't deserve this medal. The cost had been far too great. Could he give it back?

Mac got out his computer to see if there was precedent for returning medals and instead saw a note flashing. His inbox was full. He checked his email but when he noted the sender of most of them was Dave, he ignored them, though he felt like dirt for doing it. He couldn't face the man. Couldn't take his deserved condemnation. Not yet. Maybe never?

But how could he move ahead? The questions built until Mac thought he'd explode.

Is this Your plan? I'm supposed to run the Double M on my own, by myself, with no one to share the good and bad? Sure, Adele's right next door and if she adopts Francie and Franklyn they'll be there, too. My friend will be nearby. I can still see her, talk to her, but it's not the same.

She'll have the twins to love and mother and be a family with, but who will I have? Who will I share my Christmas Eves and Valentines and all the other special occasions with?

Mac had refused to allow himself to think too deeply about the future, but now he couldn't stop the questions. And with every question he asked, Adele's face filled his brain. He couldn't ask her for help, not without telling her the truth. But he desperately needed to talk to someone.

The Spenser sisters. He'd broken two appointments with them. Twice he could have sought their advice but had backed out because he was afraid they'd suggest the very thing he most feared—seeing Dave. But he had no one else to talk to.

Mac grabbed his phone and texted the sisters, asking when he could meet them. The response was swift.

Tomorrow morning, 6 a.m. at the church.

He texted back his agreement, threw the wet laundry into the dryer and switched off the lights. Tomorrow was going to be a very full day. Might as well get some shut-eye.

But as Mac lay in bed, watching fat fluffy snowflakes flutter past his window, he wondered if Tillie and Margaret would have any answers for him, or if he would simply continue to exist in this kind of limbo that now gripped him.

Don't be such a cowboy, Mac. Trust God.

Delly's chiding childhood voice echoed inside his head. He smiled as he let memories fill his head. She was such a sweetheart. If he told her the truth, would she still want him as her best friend?

Chapter Six

"Where are you two going so early?" Adele paused on the bottom step, surprised to see her aunts, wrapped in scarves and their heaviest coats, preparing to leave via the front door. "I don't know if Jake has the road plowed yet," she warned.

"He has." Did Tilly's smile look just the tiniest bit secretive?

"We asked him last night if he'd do it early this morning," Margaret explained with a glance at the grandfather clock. "We must leave now, sister. As it is we'll barely make it there on time."

"Who are you meeting at ten to six in the morning?"

Adele's questions went unanswered. Her foster aunts simply waved and walked out, quietly closing the door behind them. Adele moved to the window, watched their car pull out of the garage then head down the hill toward Chokecherry Hollow. Puzzled, she entered the kitchen.

"Don't worry, they have four-wheel drive. They'll be fine." Victoria stood by the window, holding her daughter, Grace. "Did you make coffee yet? I need several cups. This one kept me up all hours."

"I started brewing it half an hour ago when I heard the

little sweetheart crying." Adele took the little girl from her sister and jiggled a smile out of her. "Drink your coffee, Mama. I'll take over for a bit."

"Thank you." Victoria poured two mugs and then sat down at the table, smiling when Adele also sat then quickly moved her coffee out of Grace's reach. "I think the aunts are meeting Mac."

"Mac?" Adele frowned. "Why? And why this early?"

"No clue." Victoria shrugged. "But a while ago I overheard him ask if he could talk to them privately."

Victoria finished her coffee and left to give Grace her bath, and Adele got busy preparing a hearty breakfast for their visitors who would venture on a longer ride at the Double M this morning. But the entire time she cooked, served and cleaned up, her mind was busy posing questions about Mac. The feeling that something was wrong with him strengthened with every passing moment until she began to seriously consider climbing on Victoria's bus and riding over to see him with the rest of the group.

Pray instead of worrying.

So Adele did that while she opened the cooler and removed the rolls she'd started last night. She set them to rise by the stove, then began assembling ingredients for the hearty stew she'd serve for lunch. But she couldn't stop wondering about Mac. When her helper appeared, so did an idea.

"I have everything on the go," she told Stella. "Once you've baked the rolls, you can put those pans of peach cobbler in the oven. No later than eleven o'clock," she warned. "And we'll also need a veggie tray and dips."

"You're leaving?" Stella's eyes stretched wide. "But you never—" She cut off the comment, but Adele knew what she'd been about to say.

"I don't usually leave so much up to you, and I won't

go now if you think it will be too much." *Please don't say it's too much*, she prayed silently.

"I'll be fine. You go ahead." To Adele's relief, steady, reliable Stella quickly recovered her unflappable demeanor. It was one of the reasons she'd chosen this woman as her assistant. "Most everything's prepared. It's just a matter of setting the tables and stirring the stew."

"You're a peach." Adele hugged her, sending up a word of praise that God had blessed her with such a great helper. "I'm going to check my email first and then I'll head over to the Double M, just in case they need help."

"Mac McDowell—need help?" Stella huffed her disbelief. "That's new. Well, go on. I'll text you if something comes up."

"Thank you." Adele grabbed another mug of coffee, creamed it to perfection, then sat down in the study, iPad in hand, and clicked on her email. Her heart thrummed with excitement at the first one. A response from the neighbor woman who'd befriended her and Gina before foster care.

I so wish I could help you, Adele. I'd love to reconnect with Gina. But unfortunately, I have no idea of her whereabouts. I asked around the neighborhood for you but without success. Don't give up, honey. You'll find her. That's what I'm praying for.

"Me, too," Adele murmured as she closed her computer. The same old yearning and rush of sadness filled her. "Why can't I find her, God? Don't You want us to be together? Is it wrong for me to want my sister, my own flesh and blood? How can I be happy without knowing if she's okay, if she needs me, if I can help her?"

"For I have learned, in whatsoever state I am, there-

with to be content." The memory verse from a long-ago girls' club quiz reverberated inside her head.

"How do I learn to be content when I'm all alone?" she mused aloud.

"You're not 'lone, Delly." Franklyn padded over to her chair and wrapped his arms around her. "Me 'n' Francie love you. We're a fam'ly. Right?"

"Right you are." She lifted the little boy onto her knee and hugged him, relishing the just-awakened scent of him and the feel of his thin, bony arms. "I love you, too, kiddo."

Was that what God was telling her, that she needed to be content with having the precious twins in her life? Well, she was thankful for that, but somehow Adele wanted more.

"That your joy may be full." Another verse from the past. But it said what she craved. More. More family. More love. A certain special someone who would value her above all else.

Was that wrong?

"Too tight," Franklyn said, wiggling out of her arms. "I gotta wake up Francie," he announced. "We gotta get dressed."

Adele tried to remember what was significant about today.

"We're goin' to the school. 'Member, Delly? Francie's gonna tell 'bout our horse ride." He raced off, his feet thumping up the stairs as he bellowed for his sister.

Adele winced as she rose. Hopefully Victoria wasn't trying to get Grace to sleep.

She moved to the window, stared out at the snowy landscape and immediately felt guilty. She lived in this wonderful home, with fantastic people who cared about her. She was looking forward to adopting the twins, to a joyous happy Christmas. Mac was home, safe and sound. She was blessed beyond measure. What more could she ask for?

"I am thankful, God. Truly. But…"

With a sigh she thrust back that oft-suppressed yearning for someone of her own and went to prepare breakfast for the twins. Stella gave her an odd look but said nothing, smiling as the twins chattered between bites. Adele prepared their lunches then hurried them into the car.

But by the time she'd warned Francie about exaggerating, delivered the twins to their preschool in Chokecherry Hollow and picked up items Stella asked for via text, it was almost lunchtime. Adele returned to The Haven frustrated that she'd missed out on talking to Mac.

As if to add insult to injury, the handsome cowboy didn't join them for lunch. Apparently one of Mac's beloved minis had gone lame and he was waiting for the local vet to arrive. Denied the opportunity to talk to her best friend and with supper under control, Adele left Stella in charge, then went for a long cross-country ski hike, determined to sort out this sense of nagging discontent.

Mac deliberately didn't go to The Haven for lunch or for supper, though his stomach told him he was a fool. It wasn't only the lame horse that stopped him. Gabe could have seen to that. But Gabe couldn't help him accept Tillie and Margaret's early-morning advice.

"God's will isn't something you can dial into when you're ready to hear it, Mac." Margaret had given him a severe look. "You can't simply decide you need to figure out what He's planned and then expect Him to send you a vision laying it all out."

"I'd settle for a burning bush," he'd muttered in frustration and then regretted it a moment later when Tillie's tanned forehead had pleated in a frown of disapproval. "I

know, I'm not leading the children of Israel to the promised land," he'd quickly added. "But I want to do *something*
with my life and right now I feel like I'm just marking time
at the ranch. Mom and Dad will come back expecting an
answer and right now I'm no clearer on whether I'm supposed to stay here than I was when I first came home."

"So, you go on running the ranch, praying, making the
best decisions you can and watching how they turn out."
Margaret had sounded as if that was a cakewalk.

"And?" Frustration chewed at him. He far preferred
doing than being.

"If God wants you to stay on the Double M, He'll show
you. Or He'll close that door and open another," Tillie
had said.

"Meaning I'm supposed to keep working at the ranch on
the off chance I'm in the right place?" he'd asked sourly.

"There's no 'off chance,' Mac. If you're trusting God
and doing your best in the situation you're in, you're in the
right place." As Margaret read his expression her eyebrows
lifted. "You expect God to check in with you?"

"Can't you just hear how that would go?" Tillie chuckled
before dropping her voice to a low drawling tone. "'Say,
Mac, here's my idea for your life.'" Her deep, mannish tone
echoed around the sanctuary of the old church. "And then
after God lays out His master plan for you, He asks, 'Is
that okay with you, Mac, or do you have a better idea?'"

The sisters looked at each other and giggled at the ab-
surdity of it, which added to Mac's disgruntled feelings.

"We're talking about God, the one who made you and
the universe and keeps it all running together. He doesn't
need your opinion. He's the creator." Margaret had patted
his shoulder, her eyes sympathetic. "You see, that's the
thing about faith, son. Faith is trusting even though you
can't see the end result."

"But—"

"It may seem as if nothing's happening, as if you're operating in the dark. But you're not." Margaret's voice grew kindlier, more like the gentle voice in his memories of Adele's foster aunt. "You can rest assured that if you trust God, He'll work things together for His good, and yours."

"In fact, He's already doing that," Tillie had added. "Look how the children enjoy riding your horses. They were so excited at supper last night. Your ranch is such a blessing to those troubled souls who come to The Haven. Hang in there, Mac. You're doing fine."

As Mac wandered among his miniature horses in the darkness, hours after that conversation, he still struggled to accept it. No assurance, no guarantee. Just—keep on.

"But keep on with what?" he murmured.

"With what you're doing, I'm guessing." Adele smiled as he whirled around to face her. "Sorry. Didn't mean to startle you."

"It's pretty late, Delly. What are you doing here?" She looked otherworldly, with the moonlight gleaming off her white ski suit and blond hair.

"Checking up on you." Her gloved fingers smoothed over Calliope's back. "Hello, sweet thing," she murmured in a tender voice. "I'm sorry, but I don't have any sugar lumps for you."

"I don't need checking on, Adele," Mac said more gruffly than he'd intended. Maybe that was due to a surge of jealousy from the gentle cooing of her voice as she petted the animal. "I'm fine."

"Again with the *fine*." She stared at him with those see-everything amber eyes.

"Yep. Just sorting through some stuff." He shrugged and turned aside to avoid her scrutiny. "Gabe and I have decided to change the trail ride route slightly. Make it a little easier."

The way she exhaled told him she wasn't buying his diversion.

"You're not out here by yourself because of something my aunts said this morning?"

"How do you—" He shook his head. "Never mind. Someone in town saw us or your aunts told you or— It doesn't matter." Yet it did. Because he didn't want her to think he was struggling, didn't want to look weak. "I'd forgotten that living here is like living in a fishbowl."

"Actually Victoria overheard you and the aunts talking about a meeting a while ago." Adele released the horse's halter and smiled as the animal nudged her before trotting away. "But she wasn't gossiping. I saw the aunts leave and wondered where they were going so early. Did they help you?"

"Not a lot, but then perhaps I was expecting too much." Mac led the way out of the corral. "Want some coffee?"

"Peppermint tea?" She grinned at his nod and walked beside him to the house. Once inside, after shedding her outdoor gear, she walked directly to the fireplace to admire the medal. "I heard all about this. The aunts said your parents were so proud when it arrived. What exactly does *meritorious service* mean, or can't you talk about it?"

"No," he said shortly.

"Oh. Okay." Adele curled up in his dad's armchair, watching as he flicked on the kettle. "You don't have to explain about your meeting with the aunts, Mac. I don't want to pry if it's personal."

"I don't mind telling you." Was that because Adele had her own questions about God? "I'd hoped your aunts could explain how I could figure out God's will."

"Oh." She drew in her breath between her teeth. "That's a hard one. They couldn't help?"

"Basically they told me to keep on keeping on." He handed her the steaming mug, a tea bag and a teaspoon. "Not really helpful when I'm trying to figure out my future."

"But I thought—" She stopped, swallowed, frowned. "You're running the ranch. You're not staying?"

"Yes, until my parents return. But is remaining here my life's plan?" Mac shrugged. "I don't know. I thought, hoped, that once the parents had gone and I was running things, I'd feel, I don't know—confident—about staying. I'm not."

"What bothers you most?" Delly watched him, eyes huge as she sipped her tea. Obviously recognizing his struggle to explain, she urged, "Don't prevaricate. Just say it."

The one person who'd always understood when he'd shared his heart had been Adele. He dearly wanted to believe that was still true, that she'd hear him out without judging. But they'd led separate lives for so long. They'd both changed. And besides, she had her future mapped out so clearly. How could she understand?

"It's a lot to think about," he mumbled finally.

"Wimped out, huh?" Her clear-eyed gaze told him she knew he'd evaded the truth. "If you won't tell me about your struggle, can I tell you about mine?"

"Sure." Mac leaned back in his chair, waiting. He'd missed these sweet heart-to-hearts with Delly.

"Well, as you know," she began, "I thought coming back to The Haven to run the kitchen and adopt the twins was God's will for me. It was my goal."

"Was?" Mac sat up straight, frowning. "It isn't now?"

"I don't know." Tears welled and rolled down her smooth cheeks. "Everything's so difficult."

"Like what?" Mac wanted to sit on the arm of her chair, wrap his good arm around her and comfort her, but knowing Delly, this, whatever it was, needed to be said.

"I thought The Haven would be the perfect place for the twins to get over their grief, to make a new home, with me." She sniffed and wiped a hand across her cheeks.

"It isn't?" Something must have happened today. Mac mentally kicked himself for not going over for supper. Maybe he could have done something to help Delly.

"Francie and Franklyn lie, Mac. They lie all the time." Adele frowned.

"Kids do. You'll correct them and eventually they'll get over it," he said, hoping to ease her doubts.

"I don't think so." She looked straight at him. "Since coming to The Haven they've started lying about their family. Today at school Francie talked about her ride with you. Then apparently, she and Franklyn insisted that their parents would get them horses for Christmas, *when they come to get them*." Her eyes grew shiny with tears. "They were adamant about their parents' return, even later at home when I tried to talk to them."

"Huh." Mac scrambled to think of a good reason for such behavior. "Maybe they still think they're alive?"

"No." Adele's golden curls blazed under the lamp as she shook her head. "In Edmonton they knew the truth. They even talked about how God was looking after Mommy and Daddy. They asked all kinds of questions about heaven and what their parents would do there."

"I see." He ran scenarios through his mind, discarding one after another until an idea struck. "Maybe it's the preschool. Maybe they feel like they're different and they want to be the same as the other kids."

"I don't think so, Mac. I think it's me." Adele's voice had dropped to a whisper.

"You?" He brushed that off. "No way. You're the best mother—"

"They don't want me as their mom, Mac." Her voice cracked as she sobbed out the words.

"What?" He did move then, hunching down in front of her, setting aside her mug and folding his fingers around hers. "What are you talking about, Delly?"

"At bedtime tonight, Francie hugged me. And then told me she and Franklyn didn't think they could be adopted. She said her parents are coming to get them at Christmas because she prayed for that and I'd told her God always answers our prayers." Adele's face grew wet with tears. "She said they don't want me to be their mom."

"Oh, honey. I'm so sorry." Mac pulled Adele up and into his embrace, pressing her damp face against his chest as he tried to comfort her.

"If adopting Francie and Franklyn isn't God's will for me, then what is?" she wept.

Mac had no answers. All he could offer was comfort to this kind, sweet woman whose heart had just been shattered because of love for the two orphans. But starting tomorrow he was going to spend a lot more time with the twins. Because nobody would be a better mom for them than sweet Adele.

Was that why God wanted him here?

Chapter Seven

"Mac McDowell is becoming a fixture around this place," Victoria observed the following Friday, feeding Grace a bite of freshly baked shortbread.

"I think he's lonely. With his parents gone there's only Gabe for company on the ranch." Adele set the fifth pan of cookies to cool on a rack, then slid a sheet of shish kebabs into the oven.

"He's spending a lot of time with your twins, too," her sister mused.

"They're not my twins, Victoria. Not yet." *Maybe never.* The thought made her heart drop. "Anyway, I'm glad he is. Francie seems to talk more freely with Mac than anyone else."

"And Franklyn?" Victoria wiped her daughter's messy fingers.

"Franklyn mostly does what his sister wants. She's the driving force in that pair." Adele sat down to rest for a moment and sipped her coffee. "He doesn't talk about me adopting them anymore, but Francie brings it up all the time, negatively."

"It's just a phase, Adele. Eventually she'll get over what's eating her and be happy you want to adopt them.

But if their social worker drops by, we'll have to pray Francie doesn't say she doesn't want to be adopted then." Victoria must have seen Adele's shock because she quickly added, "Not that it seems like someone from Edmonton would just 'drop in.' We live in the boonies. I'm sure she'd want to make sure we'll be here if she's doing that long drive."

"I hope so." That new worry hounded Adele after her sister left and for the rest of the afternoon. Since Stella was out with the flu, she'd chosen a simple menu for supper so she could concentrate on baking as much as possible in preparation for Christmas events to which the aunties kept adding.

Intense baking sessions like this were easier done with the twins at preschool. Mac's offer to pick them up today was an added blessing. *He* was a blessing, taking over for her repeatedly since she'd bawled on his shoulder. He'd become a refuge for the twins to run to if they needed to talk. Which Francie didn't seem to be doing.

The little girl's daily insistence that she didn't want to be adopted was growing more adamant. Adele was running out of ways to figure out what was wrong.

"Please help me, God. If I'm to be their mother, I need to get this sorted out. If I'm not, well—please help me."

Stuffing away her frustration at God's lack of response to this oft-repeated prayer, Adele began mixing ingredients for the first of nine cheesecakes for the Christmas tea her aunts would host. If Adele could get the cheesecakes baked and into the freezer she might have time to help with decorating The Haven tomorrow.

"We're home." Franklyn burst through the door, grinning, eyes shining.

Home. How sweet to hear him say those words. But how sad to see Francie's crestfallen expression as she followed him, shuffling into the kitchen as if living at The Haven was a fate worse than death.

"Hi, guys. How was your day?" Adele slid a lemon cheesecake into the second oven, then smiled her thanks at Mac as he hung up the twins' coats. "You look happy, Franklyn."

"I winned the race." The little boy pulled a crumpled red ribbon out of his pocket and smoothed it out on the table before he flopped onto a chair and explained how he'd gotten first in their snow races.

"Congratulations. I think winning first deserves a snowman cookie, Franklyn." Adele set a plate with two white-frosted cookies and a glass of chocolate milk in front of him.

"Francie woulda won for best snow angel but she messed it up." The little boy glanced at her, then muttered, "On purpose."

"I hate angels." Francie's sour expression made Adele wince. She snatched a Christmas tree cookie from the plate Adele offered and, after a glance to make sure she was being watched, deliberately crushed it on the table.

Adele glanced at Mac, who shook his head. Finding no reaction from the adults, the little girl pressed her finger against the crumbs and ate them.

"I love angels." Mac sat down at the table and said cheerily, "I especially love angel cookies. May I have this one with the blue dress and silver star in her hand?"

"Help yourself." Adele offered him coffee, which he accepted with a nod before turning to Francie.

"In the Bible angels were God's special messengers, Francie." Mac's calm tone helped Adele regain her equanimity. "They told people what God wanted them to know."

"Like they tole the shepherds in the field with sheep about baby Jesus," Franklyn said.

"Exactly. I think the angels that appeared to the shepherds must have been beautiful. Like Delly." Mac studied Adele with an intensity that made her stomach flutter. "Beautiful and kind and loving."

"That's why she's gonna be our mom." Franklyn looked perfectly happy until his sister glared at him.

"She's not gonna 'dopt me." Francie smacked her glass on the table hard.

"Oh?" Mac shrugged as if it was no consequence. "Just Franklyn will be living at The Haven then. Huh." He pretended to be thinking something over. "I think I'd like to be adopted."

"You already gots a mom and dad." Francie's tone oozed scorn.

"Yes, but if they couldn't be my parents anymore, I'd want somebody else to care about me." His tone even, thoughtful, Mac studied his coffee cup, but Adele knew his words were intentionally chosen for the little girl. "Family isn't just about the people you were born to, Francie. Like Adele's aunties. She wasn't born to them. She has a mom and a dad."

Francie frowned as if this was news. "How come she don't live with them?"

"Because a long time ago her parents couldn't take care of her." Mac's smile soothed that perennial ache to belong that had hounded Adele for years. "The aunties asked if she'd come to live here. Now she's part of their family, too."

"Too?" Franklyn frowned. "What's that mean?"

"Adele still has her own mom and dad, but now she also has two aunts. Her family got even bigger when Adele met her foster sisters. Now Adele's family is really big." He munched on his cookie as if her life was utterly ordinary. "I don't have a big family. I wish I did."

"Why?" Francie's gaze was riveted to his face, as if she needed to hear the answer.

"Because it's more fun." Mac snitched another cookie as he winked at Adele. "I've always wanted brothers and sisters."

"How come?" This time it was Franklyn.

"I had a brother. His name was Carter." Adele heard the sadness in his words. "Before he got sick we played together all the time. We were best friends. But then he died, and I got lonely. I still am sometimes. If I had some other kids in my family I'd have someone to talk to and share and have fun with." Mac's stare was on something far in the past but after a moment, when Francie tugged on his arm, he returned to the present with an apologetic smile. "Yes, Francie?"

"If you 'dopted a brother it wouldn't for sure make you not sad," she said wisely.

"It wouldn't?" Mac pretended to think about that. "Maybe not. But if I had a brother we could talk about how I was sad, and we could share my minis and go riding together like I do with Delly. I think it would be fun, don't you?"

Francie shook her head in a firm *no*.

"Why not?" Mac leaned back in his chair, looking lazy and unconcerned, though Adele knew he was as eager as she to hear the response.

She was so glad Mac was here. The past few days he'd spent a lot of time with the twins when she'd been so busy she hadn't always had a chance to sit and listen. The only hitch was that whatever they discussed only seemed to make Francie more adamant that she did not want to be adopted.

"Gettin' more fam'ly don't make the hurt go 'way," Francie said in a solemn, quiet tone that pained Adele to hear.

"Nope," Mac agreed. "It doesn't. I'll always miss Carter. He had such a goofy laugh. He laughed all the time. But you know what?"

Riveted by his words, Francie and Franklyn both shook their heads.

"Carter wouldn't want me to be sad that he's not here."

Francie frowned at him, then glanced sideways at Adele, who kept icing cookies. If the child was going to confess what was bothering her, some instinct warned that Francie would have to do it on her own timetable. Adele held her breath as the little girl opened her lips as if to ask a question, then exhaled when Francie smacked them closed and crossed her arms belligerently over her thin chest.

What had she been going to reveal? Adele sighed with frustration that Mac hadn't noticed as he continued with his explanation.

"Carter's with God now and he's very happy. God has lots of things for him to do. I know Carter wouldn't ever want to come back here and be sick again, and anyway, I don't want him to."

He *had* been paying attention. Adele wanted to applaud when Francie, her attention snagged by the comment, dropped her arms and now studied Mac as if he was from Mars.

"You don't want to see your brother no more?" Franklyn frowned.

"Oh, I am going to see him again when I go to God, but that might not be for a while. But since I'm here now I know Carter would want me to be happy. And you know what?"

Franklyn, puzzled, shook his head.

"I think he'd be happy for me if I got some more family."

Mac had always talked about having a big family. Did that comment mean he was now thinking about marriage?

Funny how that thought left a sour taste in Adele's mouth as Mac pushed away his coffee cup.

"Hey, Delly, is it okay if we play that pop-up game for a while? I love that game."

"Sure." She dusted off her hands before pulling the game out of the sideboard drawer. Mac encouraged the twins to help clear off the used dishes and crumbs as Adele warned, "Be careful, though. Franklyn is very good."

"I'm better," Francie said in a truculent tone.

"Are you?" Mac's challenge made Francie blink in surprise. "Well, if either you or Franklyn beat me, I'll take you for a ride on the minis tonight. Okay?"

It was as if a switch had been thrown, Adele mused. Francie, always competitive, pursed her lips and squinted in fierce concentration as they went around and around the board. Mac led for a time, then one of the children took first place.

Adele so wanted Francie to win, wanted something to cheer up the little girl. But Francie's moves were reckless and not well thought out. She came in third just as Aunt Tillie and Margaret burst through the back door.

"Mac, help, please." Tillie was breathless, her face white. "One of the cabins is on fire."

Mac grabbed his coat and went charging out the door. Adele pressed Victoria's pager number and then Jake's. Immediately the house phone rang. Adele grabbed it, half listening to Jake, the other half hearing her aunt speak.

"We've already called the fire department, but it will take a while for them to come from Chokecherry Hollow." Margaret wrung her hands, her white face taut with worry. "There's a group down there—"

"They're fine, Auntie. Jake says Victoria took the kids and their counselors on a hike. There's no one inside the building." Adele ended her conversation with their hired man. "He has some extinguishers and Mac's there now, helping him. Why don't you go in the family room, Aunties? I'll bring you some tea."

They hurried away, anxious to pray about the situation, as they always did.

Only as she turned to put on the kettle did Adele notice Francie and Franklyn standing hand in hand, wide eyes and scared faces telegraphing their fear.

"Are Mac an' Jake gonna die like our daddy did?" Francie whispered.

"No, my darlings. We're all going to be just fine." Adele fell to her knees and drew the two into her arms, holding them tight. "We're safe. God kept us all safe. Even the boy who was playing with matches earlier."

Francie clung to her as if desperate for reassurance, but Franklyn pulled back.

"Why'd he do that?" he demanded. "Don't he know you're not s'posed to play with fire?"

"Daddy tole us that," Francie murmured.

"Maybe he doesn't have a daddy or a brother or a friend like Mac to tell him stuff like that. I'm going to need a lot of help now," she said, carefully watching their faces.

"We c'n help." Francie's chin thrust out in a determined jut. "That's what fam'lies do. They help each other. Mac said so."

"Mac's absolutely right."

"We're sorta like fam'ly, right?" The little girl was obviously struggling to make sense of her new situation. Adele's heart ached for her confusion.

"We are absolutely family, sweetheart." Adele hugged the children tightly and heaved a thank-you prayer. "There are all kinds of families and ours is a very special kind." She rose and reached for her apron. "Thank you for offering, Francie. I'd like to have some help from my very special family."

Adele assigned the twins simple tasks while she prepared tea for the aunts. Then she quickly put together enough to feed The Haven's guests, staff, family, the fire department and probably a bunch of neighbors who would soon show up to help.

As she worked, she prayed.

Keep Mac safe. Don't let him do anything foolhardy.

Because the truth was, Jake hadn't actually said Mac was okay. He'd said the rancher was trying to stop the surrounding tinder-dry woods from catching fire. Fearless, impulsive Mac.

Adele couldn't imagine life without him.

Mac wasn't exactly sure what had swayed Francie, but he had a hunch it had to do with the fire. Maybe it reminded her of her loss, maybe she thought she'd lose him or Adele. Whatever had happened, in the excitement of decorating The Haven the following day, she seemed to have forgotten her determination not to be adopted. What she hadn't lost was her affinity for questions.

"Do you like these red lights? I do. Hey, you never told us how you got hurted, Mac," she reminded as she unwound the ball of Christmas lights he was stringing over the entryway of the house. "Delly don't know neither. How come you don't tell us if we're fam'ly?"

"I—um, don't like to talk about that time, Francie." *Please, don't ask me anymore.* Mac fiddled with the arrangement even though the dangling lights followed the eaves perfectly.

"I told you 'bout my mom and dad," she said with a frown.

"I'm glad you did, Francie. I think you feel better after

talking about it, right?" He climbed down the ladder and smiled at the little girl, hoping she'd take the bait and change the subject.

"I guess. Wouldn't you feel good if you 'splained 'bout your accident?" Smart as a whip, Francie had turned the tables. "Did you do sumthin' bad? Delly said fam'lies know all 'bout you and love you anyways, even the bad parts. I'll still love you, Mac."

"Thank you, Francie. I love you, too."

The twins were such precious children. But Mac was fully aware of Franklyn and Adele arranging more lights along the hedge not ten feet away. Delly could probably hear every word they said, so he scrounged for a tactful response.

"My friend got hurt a lot worse than I did in the accident." Which was true, but only partially. Man, he hated that cloud of guilt hanging over him. "It makes me sad, so I don't like to talk about it."

"But—"

"Let's do the shrubs under the windows next, Francie. Aunt Tillie loves to see them all lit up in green." Mac kept her busy, desperate to avoid releasing any more details about the day he'd lost his arm. Maybe she'd forget about it. "You're very good at decorating, kiddo."

"Not as good as me." Franklyn grinned.

"We're all good decorators," Adele adjudicated as she stood back to admire what they'd done so far. "But we have a long way to go. My aunts have a ton of decorations."

Mac noticed another car pull in to the already-crowded driveway. Six people exited, got directions from Jake, then began erecting a massive manger scene that had been built many years earlier. All around the big stone house, friends and neighbors were helping to turn The Haven into a Christmas wonderland.

"Most of Chokecherry Hollow is here," Mac said, surprised to see them all.

"It's perfect, isn't it?" Adele's eyes shone.

"Not perfect," he corrected. "But pretty close."

"It's kind of become a tradition." She smiled at his surprise. "Several years ago my sisters and I couldn't get home early, so the townsfolk came to help the aunts put up decorations, inside and out."

"They must love seeing the house on the hill lit up at night," he mused.

"I guess so, because they now show up every year on the first Saturday in December. The aunts, of course, have turned it into a party. When everything's finished we'll serve hot apple cider, cocoa and treats. It's The Haven's way of kicking off the season of Christmas cheer." Her eyes sparkled as she grinned, her joy obvious. "Now, we need to make snowmen for the back patio. Remember doing that, Mac?"

He did remember. He remembered the laughter and the joy and the fun he'd shared with Delly, all things he'd thought he'd one day share with his own kids.

Not gonna happen now. Forget that dream, Mackenzie, his brain chided.

"I wonder how Victoria and her busload of kids from Edmonton are doing inside," he mused.

"We'll see their decor in a little while. Now, to work." She tossed a snowball at him and chuckled at his outrage before dodging his snowball. Soon the twins joined in and it was as if time had regressed. Or maybe time had advanced because he and Adele began to sound more and more like parents.

Francie, don't wash your brother's face again.

Franklyn, let Francie make her own snowman, or woman.

Mac had no experience in parenting kids and yet the correction, the chiding, the cheering—it all seemed to come naturally. That made him a little sad. He'd never have the chance to be a father now.

What's the plan for my life, God? What's in my future?

A snowball missed his nose by a centimeter. Mac let go of the questions and got busy, laughing, teasing and soaking in the sight of Adele teaching the kids about Christmas at The Haven.

As the skies dimmed to twilight, he realized he'd enjoyed the afternoon so much he'd completely forgotten about his missing arm and who was watching him. All he knew was it felt right when he and Adele sat in their snow fort watching the twins wiggle flashlights over the walls. Was this afternoon so enjoyable because when he was with Adele his problems seemed to fade away?

A call drew them to the front of the house. They'd begun decorating after lunch and at five o'clock, the big house on the hill seemed transformed. They joined the others at the front of The Haven, waiting for Jake to throw the switch. Amid gasps and sighs, the entire area twinkled and glowed. But it was when the spotlights focused on the manger scene in the center of the circular driveway with the gloriously bright star over it that everyone fell silent. Mac saw Adele brush away a tear as the group burst into a spontaneous chorus of "Away in a Manger." Then she slipped away, no doubt to check out the kitchen preparations.

Leaving the twins in the care of Jake, Mac followed. Perhaps he could help.

Help do what? Mac wasn't sure. He only knew that right now he wanted to be wherever Adele was.

"I should have been in here with you instead of playing. But you've done a wonderful job," he overheard her encourage Stella. "I could never have managed to make this dining table look so festive."

"You made it all. I just put it together," Stella demurred. "And your sister and her helper elves did the decorating. This home is so inviting already, but these old-fashioned decorations make it even cozier."

"I didn't know you did ice sculpture, Delly." As Mac stepped forward to get a closer look at the frozen multicolored Christmas tree, he accidentally brushed her shoulder. That simple contact made him catch his breath, which got stuck in his throat when she flashed her beautiful smile. "It's amazing."

"Thank you. It took hours that I should have spent on other things but—" With a grin and a shrug, Adele turned to confer with Stella about what remained to be done.

Since everything seemed well in hand, Mac intently examined Delly's work. Cookies, cakes, pies, tarts and loads of sandwiches. Each item had been presented with such attention to detail that even the colors coordinated.

"She's wasted here," he mumbled to himself.

"No, she's not, Mac." Tillie looped her arm through his companionably. "Adele's doing exactly what God created her to do, bringing joy to others by using her talents."

"Sorry. I didn't mean—" He shut up rather than cover his gaffe by lying.

"There aren't the crowds of people here that she served in Edmonton. But I believe God is using Delly to broaden our outreach." Tilly smiled. "He's using you, too."

"I'm not sure about that. The trail riders last evening really struggled. Two even fell off." And he'd felt utterly inept to stop their tumbles.

"They're fine. Struggles are part of growth. If life was a bed of roses, how would God teach us?" Tillie walked over to the huge urn on a side table and filled two cups with a rich fragrant brew that Mac identified as The Haven's famed mulled cider. "Are you more certain of God's leading now, Mac?"

"Not really," he confessed. "I'm not like Adele. I don't have one overarching goal like the twins' adoption that's driving me."

"Don't you?" Tillie sipped her cider, then tilted her head to look at him with narrowed eyes. "Isn't your goal to do God's will?"

"Well, yes, but—"

"Could be that you're already doing that on the ranch." She patted his hand. "Take it one day at a time, one struggle at a time. Open your heart to His leading and keep trusting God to show you the way."

One problem with that—his heart was closed because of the guilt.

Voices sounded in the hall.

"Ah, our guests. Will you man the punch bowl, dear? Thank you."

Mac took his place behind the massive crystal bowl and began ladling out cups of punch while his brain swirled with confusion. He'd been thinking of God's will for him in terms of one concrete idea that he could discover and carry out. But Tillie seemed to be saying that learning God's will was a process, not a destination.

"Smile, Mac. 'Tis the season. And by the way, you're standing under the mistletoe." Adele's lips brushed his in the faintest of kisses. Then she laughed as she lowered the tiny sprig of greenery she held.

Mac blinked and caught his breath. Adele was absolutely stunning in black velvet pants and a glittery black sweater that showed off her spectacular hair.

"You're beautiful, Adele." The words slipped out, a side

effect from working so hard to repress his urge to turn her little peck into a real kiss.

"Thank you, Mac." Her gaze met his and it was as if a current ran between them.

Mac couldn't explain what had changed. He only knew something had, something basic, something vital. And it scared him to death.

"I'll go check on the kids," he said quickly.

"But Jake's—"

He ignored Adele's words and hurried away, trying to order his thoughts and unable to because friends and neighbors greeted him, wanting to chat, to ask questions, to include him. He saw the twins laughing with their preschool teacher. He wasn't needed there. But there was a lineup at the beverage area.

Mac shoved aside everything and concentrated on serving drinks and helping make the party a success. Later, when he was alone, he'd sort through the miasma of reactions that filled him whenever he was around Adele. Maybe he could decipher what was happening and why.

Chapter Eight

"A man's on the phone, Delly." Francie's shrill voice carried across the kitchen. "He wants to talk to you."

"Sweetheart, you're not allowed to answer the phone. Remember?" Adele took the receiver, slightly deflated when she realized Mac wasn't the caller.

"Um, yes. I do remember you." Why would Denis Kracken be calling her? "Yes, that was Francie—oh, Mac told you about the twins. At the men's fellowship dinner last Sunday night? I see." Adele tried to be patient as the conversation stretched out, but she was preoccupied about her coconut macaroons burning. Maybe that was why she couldn't believe her ears. "Sorry? I didn't catch that. Mac said what?"

"That your engagement is off, so I was wondering if you'd like to go out for dinner."

"Uh—" Adele gulped and made the first excuse she could think of to refuse. Even so it took time for the conversation to finish. She had to move fast to rescue the macaroons, which only added to her irritation.

Mac walked through the door. And the phone rang again.

"It's 'nother man, Delly." Francie dropped the phone and raced over to Mac, regaling him with her day at preschool.

"Francie!" With trepidation, Adele lifted the phone to her ear. "Hello?"

A minute later she was refusing a second date. And then a third.

"Mac said you really need to get out," Reavis Cranch said.

"Did he? Well, that's Mac." Adele glared at the subject of her conversation. "Always exaggerating. Thanks anyway, but I'm afraid I'm just too tied up with mothering the twins and keeping the kitchen at The Haven going. Bye."

She hung up, fighting to control her temper.

"Children, I would like you to go find Aunt Tillie and ask her to tell you a story. Now," she added firmly when Francie looked ready to argue.

After one look at her face, Franklyn took his sister's hand and without a word of protest led her out of the room. Mac poured himself a cup of coffee and imperturbably sat down at the table.

"What do you think you're doing, Mac?" Adele demanded through gritted teeth. She answered the ringing phone again, said she couldn't talk now and hung up, all without looking away from him.

"Is something wrong, Delly?" His turquoise eyes couldn't look more innocent.

"Why are you trying to set me up with the male population of Chokecherry Hollow when you know very well that I have absolutely no interest in romance?" she demanded in an icy tone.

"I'm not trying to set you up," he denied. He reached out to pick up one of the macaroons that were slightly too dark, then frowned when she lifted the platter away and set it on the far end of the table, out of his reach. "I mentioned you—"

"At your men's group," she snapped, utterly frustrated.

"Yeah. I mentioned at the men's gathering that you'd broken off your engagement. Someone asked me," he added, as if to justify his actions.

"And you told them that poor little brokenhearted Adele needed male companionship. How could you, Mac?" Frustrated and feeling betrayed, Adele whipped her cake batter so hard her hand ached. "I thought you were my friend."

"I am." A second later his arm wrapped around her waist, hugging her. "You're always working here or doing something with the twins, Delly," he continued in a tender, gentler voice, his breath whisper soft against her ear. "You never take any time for yourself. I thought you might like to go out to dinner, have an adult conversation."

"So why didn't *you* ask me?" She twisted to stare into his eyes mere inches from hers and saw his face tighten at the question before he quickly moved away, taking the warmth of his arm with him.

"Because I want you to think about what you're giving up by remaining so dead set against marriage. Not every romantic relationship is like your parents'," he insisted just before he bit into a macaroon.

"My mother is engaged again, did I tell you? For the fifth time. Still hoping for Mr. Right." Adele bit her lip as she poured the batter into individual muffin cups and set them to bake. Then she faced him, determined to make him understand. "You know that my decision is not a whim or something I'm going to *get over*, Mac. I am not interested in romance. Period." She paused to see if her words were sinking in.

"But you're alone—"

"Really? The Haven is always teeming with people—

my sister and her family, the aunts. And we constantly have guests." She met his stare head-on. "Aside from the trail riders, I doubt you get a lot of visitors at the Double M. Would you like me to suggest the single ladies in town give you a call?"

"No!" He looked aghast but recovered quickly. "It's not the same."

"Why isn't it?" she demanded, hands on her hips.

"I've just started running the ranch. I don't have time—"

"Ditto." She arched one brow and waited.

"It is different," he persisted. "I lost my arm. I'm hardly a prize catch. Anyway, it's going to take a while for me to adjust—"

"Mac McDowell, do not finish that sentence." Utterly exasperated, Adele smacked her wooden spoon on the counter and marched over to stand in front of him. "You manage perfectly well without your arm and we both know it. You *have* adjusted. The trail rides are going well. Our clients love them. Your herd is fine, according to Gabe." She tilted one eyebrow. "From my perspective, a little female companionship could only enhance your world."

"Volunteering?" he said with his lopsided grin.

"Mac. I'm your friend but your efforts to matchmake for me are unwanted, unnecessary and utterly futile. If you persist, our friendship will suffer. Clear?" Flustered by his refusal to accede, she flopped onto a kitchen chair and sipped her now-cold coffee.

"A man could add a lot to your world."

"You did not just say that to me," she snapped. Mac had the grace to blush.

"What I meant was—"

"Back off." She glared at him.

Mac's voice was very quiet, very stern. "The twins need a father."

"We're gettin' a new daddy?" Francie stood in the doorway, holding Aunt Tillie's favorite mug. "Who?"

"When?" Franklyn asked from behind her.

"You did this," Adele growled. "You fix it." She rose, found Stella in the next room preparing for the aunts' cheesecake tea. "Can you remove the cream puffs from the oven in ten minutes?"

When Stella nodded, Adele grabbed her coat, hat, and gloves, tugged on her boots and stomped outside with absolutely no idea where to go. Seeing Victoria's trekking groups had worn a path over the snow down to the creek, she followed it, fuming at Mac.

December's first balmy days had now been usurped by frigid arctic air that blasted her cheeks and drove her to seek the shelter of a piney grove set back from the edge of the frozen water. Adele sank onto a granite boulder and drew her knees to her chest, trying to rationalize Mac's disloyalty.

"He's always been my best friend, always understood my determination to avoid romance. How could he make me a laughingstock of the whole town?" Maybe she already was? Maybe these men wondered why she wasn't involved? Mac's suggestions would have only added to the speculation. "After so many years, how could he understand me so little?"

She didn't know how much time had passed when the hesitant voice drew her from her introspection.

"Delly?"

"Go away, McDowell."

"I can't. I'm really sorry but we can't talk about that now."

"Why not?" She kept her back to him. "You know how I feel. You know what I've decided."

"Yes, I know. I messed up and I'm sorry. I won't do it

again, I promise." He sounded remiss, though something else underlay his words. "Delly, you have to come to the house. Now."

Something in his voice, in his face, made her turn and study him. "Why?"

"There's a social worker there and Francie is telling her all about how she's getting a daddy for Christmas." Mac had the grace to look ashamed. "I'm really sorry."

"You should be." With a sigh, Adele grasped his hand as they climbed up the hill. "When this woman leaves, you and I are going to have a discussion, Mac."

"Okay." He didn't argue. He simply kept going until they'd reached the summit. "Why is she here now? Today? I don't like this."

"Neither do I, but nobody asked my opinion." Adele walked toward the house with a sinking heart, wondering if the woman was here to take away the twins.

"The aunts would tell us to trust God." Mac's troubled voice held foreboding. "You don't mind if I take off after I make sure everything's okay, do you? I'm going home to pray."

"You should have done that before you tried to set up my love life," she grumbled. Her fingers curled around the doorknob as trepidation filled her. "Go now," she urged. She pushed open the back door, then twisted her head toward him and whispered, "Pray hard, Mac. Please?"

"I promise." He brushed his lips against hers and then hurried toward his truck. Adele stepped into the kitchen while her heart pleaded with God for help.

"An' Delly wants to 'dopt us so Mac c'n be our daddy."

Francie's words sent a shaft of longing to Adele's heart. She was going to have to examine that later, too.

"Hello, Enid. I wasn't expecting you today." Adele slid out of her outdoor clothes as she smiled at the woman who could make or break her plea to adopt the twins. "I see you have some coffee. Why don't we go into the family room to chat?"

She'd been going to ask Stella to watch Francie and Franklyn, but Enid encouraged them to come along.

"Tell me about this new beau of yours," she said when they were both seated in the aunts' armchairs in front of the roaring fire. "Mac, isn't it? He's certainly handsome."

"He's an old friend, my first one when I came to The Haven. He was recently injured and is home to recuperate." Adele winced at Francie's bright eyes, recognizing the look she got when she was about to fantasize. She tried to interest the kids in playing the game that sat on Aunt Margaret's desk, to no avail.

"Mac crashed his plane, that's how he got hurted. His friend got hurted badder but Mac don't like to talk 'bout it." Francie flopped on the rug at their feet and frowned. "He's gonna be the bestest daddy."

"Oh, congratulations—"

"Francie. Mac isn't going to be your daddy," Adele said, heart sinking.

"But you didn't like none of them other men." Franklyn frowned, face puzzled.

"My word, it sounds as if you've been busy." Enid's eyes grew wide. "I didn't realize you're so eager to get married, Adele. I thought you'd said you would be trying to adopt as a single woman."

"I am. I will be." *Oh, Lord, please help me straighten out this mess.*

"If that's the case, it's not wise to let the children think otherwise." Disapproval leeched through every word.

"Enid, you and I need to talk privately. I'll be back in a moment. Excuse me. Come, children." Adele grabbed the hand of each child and drew them from the room, maintaining her hold when Francie tried to resist as they climbed the stairs. She tapped on Victoria's bedroom door, explained and asked her to tell the children a story. A long one. "Francie and Franklyn, you are not to leave this room until I come to get you."

Met with surly silence, Adele thanked her sister, then returned to Enid.

"I'm sorry. There's been a mistake. Let me explain," she began.

"You don't have to. Francie is making up stories again, isn't she?" Enid scribbled something in the file on her lap. "I'd thought—hoped—you were making progress with that."

"I was. But they've come to love Mac and have obviously misunderstood our friendship. Mac isn't interested in marriage any more than I am. We're good friends, but only friends."

Only friends? Was that really all she felt for Mac—friendship?

Could friendship explain the way her pulse had thudded when he'd kissed her less than half an hour ago? Was it friendship that made her heart gallop when she waited to catch sight of him every time she visited the ranch or when he came here?

Or had their friendship changed—on her part at least?

"How did it go?" Mac threw his gloves on a nearby bench after inviting Adele and the twins into his ranch house. "I was up most of last night, thinking and praying for you."

"Thanks." Adele waited at the kitchen table until the twins were busy playing with the puppies in front of the fire. "It didn't go well. Enid, the social worker, doesn't like that Francie's still making up stories, especially stories about getting a father. Namely you."

"Me?" Aghast, Mac froze. "I never said that!"

"No. But Francie extrapolates from what she hears. According to some psychiatrist Enid sent her to a while ago, Francie needs certainty in her life. When she feels uncomfortable she makes up stuff." Delly looked at him with that familiar impervious amber stare. "I had a terrible time explaining to Enid about those men calling for a date. I'm sure she thinks I'm flighty."

"I doubt it." He scoffed at the very idea.

"Mac, I'm trying to adopt." She frowned at him. "I need things on an even keel. No changes, nothing that could unsettle Francie or Franklyn."

"Right." He poured some peanuts into a dish and gave them to the twins after a warning against feeding the nuts to the puppies. Then he started the coffee maker. No change? No excitement? That was so not his world and he hated the thought that she would settle for it, but for Delly's sake he would not cause problems.

"By the way, the other day when we were hanging lights…" Adele paused as if she were struggling to recall something. "You and Francie were talking about your accident. Yesterday she mentioned it again. I didn't realize your friend had been injured at the same time as you. Was he your copilot?"

"Yes." Mac was relieved his back was turned. It gave him a chance to school his features into a blasé mask before he faced her and held out a cup of coffee. "The twins are learning to ride very quickly. Won't be long before the minis aren't enough for them."

"Mac." Adele stopped him from opening a pack of store-bought cookies he'd put on the table by the simple expedient of placing her hand over his. "I'll listen if you want to talk about it."

"I don't." He pulled away his hand and dumped the cookies onto a plate. His skin burned under her touch. Mac quickly picked up his cup. "Ever."

"Why is it such a secret?" Adele had never given up easily. Why would she now?

"It's not a secret. I simply don't want to rehash every morbid detail. It happened. Moving on." He shrugged as if it was of no consequence, when the truth was he couldn't erase the guilt of knowing he was at fault.

"Your copilot, what was his name?"

"Dave," he told her through gritted teeth. Immediately an image flashed of the day he'd gone to see his buddy. He'd stood in the doorway of Dave's hospital room and stared at the damaged shell of a weeping man who'd previously insisted nothing could happen to him that God didn't allow.

God had allowed Mac to make Dave a paraplegic? Guilt and shame haunted him as he remembered how he'd left the hospital without even talking to the man who'd been his best friend ever since he joined up. How was that action worthy of a medal?

"Mac?" Adele's soft voice pulled him back through the dark cloud of dishonor. "I'm only trying to understand."

"What's to understand?" he demanded bitterly. "I lost my arm and Dave—got hurt. Excuse me." Mac had to leave before he told her everything. He took a few moments to settle his thoughts, then returned through the living room, smiling at the twins' shrieks of delight as the puppies tumbled over the carpet. "They're cute, aren't they?" he said, squatting beside Franklyn.

"They sure getted big fast." The little boy cuddled a ball of brown fur against his cheek. "This one is Fudgey."

"This one is Kisses 'cause he's always kissing me." Francie giggled as a pink tongue darted out to touch her nose.

As the children shared the simple joy of puppies, something inside Mac ached. Losing his best buddy, losing his hand—those weren't the only casualties of his reckless actions. Now he would never be a dad, never have a home filled with laughing kids, never have a son named Carter to honor his brother.

Mac craved the same joy the twins knew, an inner peace that would override his past and release him from the dark cloak of guilt. He'd prayed for that many times. But how could anyone forgive what he'd done, what he'd left uncorrected for all these months?

Mac stood and walked back to the table where Delly waited.

"I'm sorry," she murmured.

"For what?" He pretended nonchalance. Pretense had always been his go-to for managing life's hard parts. "I know everyone's curious about the accident, but I do not want to discuss it."

"Okay." But Adele's pensive expression and darkening irises told him she was not okay with that.

"Gabe and I planned a kind of rodeo for the kids tomorrow. Want to hear?" When she nodded, Mac launched into a drawn-out explanation of their ideas.

True to form, Adele applauded their concepts and made valuable suggestions that would enhance the experience for the children. That was the thing Mac loved most about Adele, that ability to stand apart and visualize things through the innocent eyes of a child.

"How's Francie doing with the actual adoption idea?" he asked curiously.

"She was gung ho when she thought she was getting a

daddy." Pursed lips told him Adele was still irritated by his actions. "After I explained that wasn't going to happen, she went silent. She's not saying yes, but she's stopped saying no." Delly sighed. "There's something going on inside that head. I can't quite puzzle it out."

"Sooner or later she'll tell you," Mac promised.

"I hope it's before the social worker visits again. I don't want to juggle another bombshell with Enid watching." Adele's hands twisted and untwisted.

"Surely you're not questioning your abilities?" He couldn't believe it. "Delly, you're going to be a fantastic mother to these two. You already are."

"I'm not so sure about that." She lifted her head to glance at him. Her blond curls caught the light, enhancing their golden sheen. "There are so many things to get a handle on, things the books don't tell you. Not only about the twins but about life, or my life as it would be with them."

"How do you mean?" Mac leaned back, knowing she needed to say this and that he needed to listen, to offer support.

"What if something happened to them? How can I keep them safe? What if I fail them? What if I make huge mistakes that scar them forever?" She poured out a litany of fears. She paused, then whispered, "What if I can't adopt them?"

"Adele." Shocked that this confident, self-assured woman doubted herself so much, Mac cupped her chin in his hand and gently forced her to look at him. "No parent has all the answers. Ask Victoria. The main thing is you love the kids and do your best for them." He chuckled as he let go of her, fingertips immediately missing the velvet touch of her skin. "My mom always said she made it up as she went along and trusted God to fill in for her shortcomings."

"Yes, but she was your real mother, not an almost stranger." Adele sniffed back her emotions.

"You're not a stranger to Francie and Franklyn. You're the one who makes their world make sense." *You do the same for me.* "Delly, maybe it's time for you to push for more than mere custody of the twins." Mac wasn't sure this was the right answer. He knew only that he couldn't stand to watch his friend sink into a chasm of doubt and fear when adopting these kids was her heart's desire.

"You mean, I should push forward my petition for adoption?" She frowned. "I thought it would be better to wait and let the court see I'm capable and serious."

"What would show you're serious more than making your intent so clear they can't ignore it?" Mac loved the way her amber eyes began to glow as she considered it. This woman had such a big heart. "You're not going to settle for simply being their foster mother. You want permanent custody. You want the right to make all the decisions in their lives."

"You think I'm up to that?" she whispered. "Really, Mac? You don't think I'm shortchanging them by not giving them a father?"

"You will never shortchange Francie and Franklyn, Adele." Mac knew that as well as he knew his own name. "Anyway, if you change your mind, you can always add a husband later," he teased.

She glared at him, but Mac didn't respond. Suddenly he was too busy concealing his negative reactions to thoughts of some guy coming between him and Adele.

Of course, he wanted her to be happy. But when he'd told those guys to call her, Mac hadn't really thought about how a man in Adele's life would affect *him*. She'd naturally turn to the other man, he now realized. And he'd lose his best friend.

That thought made him want to yell "No!"

Chapter Nine

"You and Ben still aren't speaking to each other?"

Adele couldn't suppress the niggle of worry that had begun building last night after her foster sister had sat stony-faced through dinner, in obvious avoidance of her husband. Her stomach twisted at the very thought of *this* marriage faltering.

"No." Victoria avoided her gaze and sipped her early-morning coffee while her daughter played with a toy.

Adele's stomach sank. If Victoria and Ben could fall out of love— "Anything I can do?"

"No. I'm waiting for him to apologize." Victoria's lips pursed. "He challenged me on my decision to let a trouble-making kid go riding with the rest of the group this afternoon. He said I'm putting the other kids in danger. Which is utterly ridiculous."

"Is it?" Adele saw irritation alter Vic's face and quickly backtracked. "I'm not taking Ben's side, Vic. I'm just wondering if maybe he noticed something you didn't."

"Nothing concrete, he says. A 'feeling.'" Her expression showed exactly how she felt about Ben's feeling. She glanced at Adele, then frowned. "Stop looking like that."

"Like what?"

"As if you expect us to end up in divorce court over this. People disagree, Adele. It's normal and even healthy." She shrugged. "We'll talk it out and be fine. I just need a bit of time."

"Okay." Adele busied herself assembling ingredients for breakfast waffles. Her sister left the kitchen with a refilled cup of coffee. Half an hour later she heard Ben, Victoria and their kids leaving via the front door. She peeked out the window and saw them hand in hand, strolling down the driveway for their usual early-morning walk, and heaved a sigh of relief that there was no obvious sign of strife.

"Are you dreaming about Christmas, dear?" Aunt Margaret entered and poured herself a coffee.

"More like watching Ben and Vic. They had an argument." She suddenly felt guilty for repeating that.

"So did Tillie and I. She wants to go downhill skiing. I think it's too dangerous. At her age—at *our* ages—we shouldn't take silly risks." Frustration tightened Margaret's lips.

Adele couldn't help staring. She'd seldom if ever heard the aunts disagree. To see Margaret's irritation now was upsetting.

"Why are you frowning, dear?" Margaret asked.

"It's just— I'm surprised. I've never heard you and Tillie argue."

"Well, we do. She's a daredevil and that disturbs me." Her aunt plunked the cream pitcher on the table as if to emphasize her words. Then she sighed. "I'll get over it. I always do."

"Oh." Adele wasn't sure what to say.

"I recall how arguing always bothered you. You always wanted harmony and peace. But some disagreement is healthy, Adele. Everyone has an opinion and to keep silent just to avoid an upset isn't necessarily good. We must express our feelings and trust the ones we love will respect us for them," Margaret murmured. "As we must respect theirs."

"I guess." Adele didn't like this conversation. Quarreling always reminded her of her parents' bitter feuds and how afraid she'd been as they escalated.

"You see, dear, it's all in how you disagree. From the little you've told us in all these years, I doubt your parents disagreed with respect. They just vented and let their anger pour over the other person with no concern for their feelings. That demeans the other person. It doesn't allow for their thoughts and feelings." Margaret sipped her coffee but was clearly not finished. "If you love someone, you owe it to them to listen to what they have to say just as they owe it to you to do the same. Meanness of spirit has no place in disagreements. It all boils down to *how* you love others."

"I understand, Auntie." Adele spotted their campers tromping up the hill toward The Haven and checked on the frying bacon.

Maybe Aunt Margaret was right. Problem was Adele only remembered her parents' *claims* of love. They *said* the words, but their actions didn't show love. Her mother had *claimed* to love each successive husband, too, but those relationships had ended in bitter divorce. Sort of like the way Rafe had *claimed* he loved her and then lied to her.

But Victoria's laughter and Ben's full-bodied chuckle as they reentered the house a while later proved their quarrel had been resolved or at least tabled. Maybe their marriage was one of the few that could allow and survive arguments. For now anyway.

As she poured the waffle batter onto her griddle, Adele wondered if arguing would quash her new and unexpectedly tender feelings for Mac. Those were definitely *not* the best-friend kind of feelings.

"Delly?" Francie tugged on her apron to get her attention.

"Good morning, sweetie. You look nice." But Adele saw trouble brewing in the little girl's dark eyes.

"No, I don't." Francie's arms crossed over her thin chest. "Franklyn said I'm fat. Franklyn's stupid and mean." Tears welled.

"Am not. And you are so too fat for that dress." Thunderclouds roiled in Franklyn's eyes. "Dummy."

Adele heaved a sigh. More disagreements. Perfectly normal, Victoria and Aunt Margaret had both said. Which probably meant there'd be more of this in her future.

"That's enough from both of you. We will not start our morning with nasty words." Adele raised her eyebrows at both children. With a sigh they grudgingly apologized to each other. "Good. Now let me look at both of you. Oh, I see the problem."

"What problem?" Francie demanded, smoothing her skirt.

"Sweetie, you and Franklyn have both grown. Your dress is a bit tight, just as Franklyn's pants are a bit short. We need to get you some new clothes."

"A Christmas dress?" Francie's eyes expanded, her interest tweaked. "Sparkly like your top?"

"And c'n I get black pants like Mac's?" Franklyn added. "With cowboy boots?"

"If Stella can stay late today, we'll check out the stores this afternoon for *school* clothes. Okay?" With that issue settled, the twins plunked down on chairs at the table and began eating breakfast.

Stella arrived moments later, agreed to work late, and immediately began serving Adele's fluffy waffles and a multitude of fruits and syrups to the young guests who were filing into the dining room. For a moment Adele's world was at peace.

Then Mac burst through the back door.

"Delly, I've got the most fabulous idea," he said in the most excited tone she'd heard from him in ages. "You have to hear me out."

Her heart gave a jump for joy at the sight of him and her eyes couldn't help lingering on his handsome face as her heart lifted. So much for peace and quiet.

"Good morning, Mac. Have a seat. We're just serving breakfast." She smiled and set a fully loaded plate on the table for him. At least she and Mac would never argue so hard it would fracture their friendship.

Suddenly her day seemed much brighter.

"It's an amazing idea and I do want to hear more," Adele said in a rushed tone. "But I have to take the twins to preschool now."

"Yeah. Okay." Mac was disappointed. "I guess I have a trail ride to lead, too." He thanked Stella when she cleared away his plate. "Maybe I could pick up the twins after school. We could talk after that."

"No!" Francie glared at him. "That's when we're goin' shopping for my Christmas dress. Delly promised."

"I promised we'd go shopping, Francie. I didn't promise anything about a dress," Adele corrected. He guessed she didn't want to divulge her secret sewing project for the twins just yet.

"Shopping. Oh." Not his favorite activity.

"After that we have practice for the kids' Sunday school program." Adele thought a moment, then suggested, "Later this afternoon?"

"Gabe and I have to, um, fill a beef order," he said with a sideways glance at the twins. "But maybe after supper, if we're finished."

"Hmm. This group is leaving after their ride with you,

but the church youth are coming for a sledding party tonight," she mused aloud. "I have to be here to feed them. I can't ask Stella to stay that late. Anyway, I'll need her help with the dinner tomorrow night. The aunts always host it for the church choir. Text me," she said. "Meanwhile I'll muse on your new idea for a daylong ski clinic."

Mac saw her glance at the clock before urging the children to get their coats on. Knowing he couldn't hold them up, he followed them out.

"You really think Victoria will go for a daylong ski outing?" he asked when Adele finished belting in the kids.

"We'll plan every detail so well she'll have no doubts. Gotta go. See you." She waved at him before driving away.

Restless, Mac played with Spot and Dot for a few minutes, throwing sticks they could fetch, laughing as they rolled in the snow as part of the game. Finally he walked to his truck, wishing he could get Delly's input now. It struck him then that she was becoming more and more important in his plans.

"Yoo-hoo, Mac!" Tillie and Margaret's faces were rosy with the cold—they were obviously returning from their morning walk. "Can we have a moment of your time?"

"Sure." He followed them into The Haven, wondering what this conversation would be about. Once he'd hung their coats and his own, he trailed them into the family room, shrugging when Stella blinked in surprise at his reappearance. "How are you, ladies?"

"We're wonderful," Tillie exclaimed, eyes shining. "God is good."

"Please, sit." Margaret waved toward a chair, though she and Tillie claimed the wingbacks closest to the fire. "We wondered how you're doing, dear. Are you feeling closer to understanding God's will for you?"

"We've been praying for that for you, Mac." Tillie folded her hands and leaned forward to listen.

"Thank you. I'm not certain that what I'm doing is God's plan for my future," he began, struggling to organize his thoughts. "But so far the trail rides seem to be very popular."

"Very." Margaret smiled, then leaned her head sideways in a gesture for him to continue.

"Adele has helped me refine my general ideas and tailor each ride for the specific groups. I actually came over today to discuss a new idea I've had." They looked at him expectantly. "I thought perhaps the older kids who come here needing a challenge might enjoy a daylong ski event through the woods."

"Fantastic." Tillie clapped her hands together, her excitement obvious.

"Are you sure you can handle it?" ever-practical Margaret asked.

"Gabe and I are going to do a couple of practice runs to make sure," Mac explained, knowing the ladies were always concerned about the safety of their guests.

"Excuse me." Tillie pulled her chiming phone out of her pocket and read the text. With a frown she passed her phone to Margaret.

"Oh, dear." Margaret handed the phone back but said nothing more.

Suddenly uncomfortable, Mac hesitantly explained, "I'm hoping that tonight I can get Adele's input on a couple of things to perfect my plan."

The aunts glanced at each other, faces telegraphing something he didn't understand.

"Is something wrong?"

"Adele might be unavailable for a bit." Tillie sounded sad.

"Why?" Immediately Mac's radar went on high alert. "The twins?"

"Gina." Margaret sighed. "That was Adele's text. She just received a phone call with more disappointing news about locating her sister. We're to ask Stella to take over for a while. Adele said she needs some time off this morning."

For Adele to deliberately escape cooking—Mac had never heard her do that before. Which meant his best friend had been decimated by whatever she'd just learned. He bit his lip, wishing he'd been nearby to at least comfort her.

"On the other hand, thinking about your idea might be just the thing to take our girl's mind off her troubles," Tillie murmured thoughtfully.

"Perhaps it would. Momentarily." Margaret sighed. "It's so frustrating that she can't find out anything about Gina. I wonder what God's doing. And how we can help."

"Remember, sister, James said, 'If any of you lack wisdom, let him ask of God, that giveth to all men liberally, and upbraideth not; and it shall be given him.' Let's go ask him." Tillie patted Mac's shoulder. "You'll excuse us, won't you, son? It's time we prayed for our Adele."

"I have to go, too." Mac drove to the ranch, deep in thought. The aunties wanted to help Adele, but so did he. He was supposed to be her best friend. There had to be something he could do.

He walked inside the house for a cup of coffee and to think. Spying his Bible, he recalled Tillie's comments. He grabbed it and thumbed through the pages until he came to the first book of James. Verse five was the portion Tillie had quoted. He read further.

"But let him ask in faith, nothing wavering."

Okay, that was clear enough. If Mac wanted to help Adele, he could ask God to show him how. But what if… His eyes riveted on the last part of verse six.

"For he that wavereth is like a wave of the sea driven with the wind and tossed."

Was that what was wrong with his prayers? That he hadn't truly expected God would answer him, would show a way to be free from the load of guilt he carried, a way to run the ranch the way God wanted, to be Adele's good friend?

"I have to do something to help her. She's helped me so often, cheering me on, encouraging me when I didn't think I could do it. She always comes up with great ideas that enhance mine."

For a few minutes Mac let himself enjoy the flutter of joy inside that thoughts of this special woman always brought. Each day he cherished their times together more, so much so that he couldn't fathom not always having Adele in his world, in his corner.

And when she knows the truth about your "accident?" his brain prodded. *When she understands that this so-called best friend of yours still hasn't heard your apology? That you haven't even bothered to see him? That you have a medal you don't deserve? That you've never owned up to causing that accident?*

Adele would be appalled by his silence. Mac could visualize disappointment filling those amber eyes, feel her pain as she tried to hide her disenchantment with him. He could almost feel the empty chasm yawning inside when she began avoiding him.

Just thinking about Adele not being there was like a knife to the heart. And yet, he couldn't tell her the truth. Not yet.

Instead Mac bowed his head and asked for God's leading, so they could find Gina. He'd barely breathed the prayer when the name of his buddy who did private investigation flickered through his mind. Though almost certain the guy was still unavailable, Mac decided to text him and ask for ideas on how to locate Adele's long-lost sister on their own. For a moment his faith wavered, but he gritted his teeth and repeated the ending of verse six. *"For he that wavereth is like a wave of the sea driven with the wind and tossed."* That was James's advice.

Mac was pulling on his boots moments later when his phone chimed.

Simplest thing is to place an ad in big city papers asking for information.

Calling himself an idiot for not having thought of it, Mac paused. This was an answer to his prayer. It wasn't about him; it was about God showing him what to do. Heart lightening, he abandoned his boots and went to his computer, where he composed a short ad giving his email address if anyone had information.

Satisfied that he'd finally found a concrete way he could help Delly, Mac pulled on his outerwear and hurried to assist Gabe with this afternoon's riders. But though he worked hard to keep his mind on the youth and his horses, Mac couldn't dislodge the niggling voice inside his head.

You're still hiding the truth. Helping Adele won't be enough when she finds out who you really are.

"It was a great afternoon. Thank you, Mac. The kids really enjoyed it. Too bad Adele couldn't make it. The ice fishing idea was hers," Victoria said three days later, ushering the last of the stragglers onto the bus. Then she followed them, waved and drove away.

Gabe scrutinized his face. "Something wrong, boss?"

"Boss?" Mac shook his head. "Hardly. And no, but why do you ask?"

"Your brain's been somewhere else all afternoon." Gabe shrugged. "I've got a hunch it has something to do with your phone. Go do what you need to. I'll make sure the horses are okay."

"Thanks, Gabe." Mac grinned at him. "The ice fishing *was* a hit, wasn't it?"

"Yeah." Gabe grimaced. "If you don't count having to clean them."

"You lost the coin toss, remember? I'll see you in a while." Mac gave a half wave then hurried toward the house. The afternoon edition of the newspaper with his ad in it had been delivered. He could hardly wait to check his email and see if there was an answer today.

With a cup of hot coffee in hand, he sat down in front of the computer and logged in.

Nothing.

He checked multiple times all through the evening, skipping dinner at The Haven, desperate to do something, anything, to help Adele find Gina. Finally, after one last check before retiring, he had two replies. One was useless, but the other suggested he contact a youth center in Edmonton where the person thought they'd heard the name.

It was late. No one answered the phone, of course.

Mac spent the night stewing, wondering, tossing as he prayed over and over for God to help him solve Adele's dilemma. Maybe if he found Gina, Delly would be so overjoyed to meet her sister she'd overlook his lack? Doubtful, but he would track this lead as far as it would go.

Mac was up early and completed his chores long before early-riser Gabe even appeared. He ignored the foreman's surprise and ate his breakfast while waiting for the clock to tick past nine. Finally Mac pulled out his cell phone and dialed. Then he held his breath.

"Edmonton Youth Center," a woman's voice answered.

"Hi. I am trying to locate a woman called Gina Parker. Her family would very much like to reunite with her." Mac inhaled. "I was told that she might be at your center. Is that correct?"

"Parker. The name's not familiar but I'm sorry, I'm not at liberty to give more information over the phone."

"But I need to know for sure. May I speak to whomever can tell me? It's very important." *Please, God, please help Adele.*

"One moment." He heard a shuffling noise, then the voice asked, "Can you take this call?"

A moment later a man's voice, a voice Mac knew all too well said, "This is Dave. How may I help you?"

Mac froze.

"Hello? Are you there?" The husky voice softened. "Tell me what you need. Maybe I can help."

Slowly, carefully, Mac hung up. He set the phone on the table and stared at it.

Why was Dave at a youth center?

You got dreams, Mac? I do. Someday I'm gonna finish my degree and work with kids. I always wanted that, but university is so expensive.

Dave. His former copilot. If Mac spoke to Dave, his buddy would recognize his voice.

Mac had never apologized for causing the accident, never wished his buddy a speedy recovery, never asked if there was anything he could do to help. Mac had run away from that responsibility just as he'd spent most of his life running away from life's hard parts.

He could hardly call and ask Dave about Gina. Not that it was likely she was there, according to the receptionist. But then why did he get that lead? And what were his choices now? Take Adele to this center, face Dave, be castigated and shamed in front of her? No!

But denying Adele the chance to find her sister was unbearable. Both were impossible choices.

"Mac?" Gabe stuck his head in the door. "We've got to round up those steers for market now."

"Be right there." Mac rose, dressed in his warmest clothes and grabbed a light snack to eat while they were in the west pasture. He saddled his horse and headed out to the roughest territory on the Double M. As he and Gabe corralled the selected animals, Mac put everything else on the back burner.

He'd think of a way to give Adele this maybe-lead about her sister later.

Chapter Ten

There was something seriously wrong with Mac.

As they sat beside each other in church, Adele couldn't help noticing that he didn't sing the Christmas carols with his usual gusto. He'd also missed dinner the last two nights and appeared to have forgotten all about his latest idea of a daylong ski venture when she'd brought up the subject this morning before the service began.

What was going on with her best friend?

"Today marks the second Sunday of Advent," the pastor said as he closed his sermon. "The wise men probably didn't arrive until long after the birth of Jesus but consider their gifts. Gold, frankincense and myrrh. Not practical gifts like diapers or baby food. But gifts fit for a king. What will your gift to God be this Christmas? Humility? Thoughtfulness? Sacrifice?"

Troubled by Mac's odd behavior, Adele struggled to pay attention to the pastor's comments. She rose slowly when the congregation was dismissed. Mac remained seated.

"Congratulations, you two." The pastor's wife beamed at them.

"Uh, thanks." Adele glanced at Mac, who rose, appearing just as confused as she felt. "For what exactly?"

"On your engagement, of course. It's wonderful, and of course, none of us had any idea you two were even dating." The woman gushed on about weddings and future children. Adele was too stunned to interrupt.

"Wait." Mac seemed to have finally broken free of his daze. "What did you say?"

"Francie and Franklyn told us all this morning. We're so—" Suddenly the woman's expression altered. She glanced at Adele's bare ring finger then sighed. "They were making it up, weren't they?"

"I'm afraid so. Mac and I aren't engaged. We're just friends." Adele tamped down her irritation with the twins to glance at her *friend*, who appeared more stunned than angry. "I've been working hard to correct the twins' habit of these fabrications. In fact, I thought they'd accepted—"

A lineup of people had formed behind the pastor's wife, all of them bearing knowing grins.

"Oh, no." Adele hated the attention that denying the engagement would bring. Why had the twins done it and how could she make them truly understand that she wasn't marrying anyone, that they wouldn't have a new daddy? Why now?

"Sorry everyone." Mac's raised voice echoed around the sanctuary. "The story isn't true so there's no need for congratulations. Adele and I are just friends."

Confusion mixed with surprised murmurs filled the room. Then, smiles sagging, the group melted away, leaving her and Mac alone.

"Let's go get them." Adele picked up her purse and stepped into the aisle. As she did, her heel caught on the rug. Before she could topple over, Mac's arm slid around her waist and held her as she regained her balance.

And suddenly, in that moment, Adele wished the twins had been telling the truth, that she and Mac were engaged to be married, that they could give Francie and Franklyn their dream of a family. Truthfully, in her heart of hearts, Adele wanted exactly what other young couples took for granted: the pure simple gift of love from someone who supported you and cherished you and made each moment part of a lifetime of love.

Only—she didn't love Mac. Did she?

Even if these odd stirrings inside could be called love, what would happen to the twins when that love faded, died?

Because that was what love did.

"Adele? You okay?" he asked when she didn't pull away.

"Uh, yeah. Thanks." She gathered her composure to face the people still milling around the foyer. Then Mac's hand covered hers, shattering her serenity with such a rush of longing she was afraid to look at him for fear he'd see. Where had this need come from?

"Don't be too hard on them, please, Delly."

"How can you say that?" she asked. "They've embarrassed us badly."

"Francie and Franklyn are only going after what they want, in the only way they know," he murmured. "They're trying to control their world, a world that hasn't made any sense since they lost their family. I don't want to see them crushed, not so close to Christmas."

"Then I think you should be there when I explain you and I aren't getting married." She expected him to refuse, to make an excuse. But Mac simply shrugged.

"I'd like to tell them, if you don't mind."

Adele was so surprised by his take-charge attitude that it took a moment to gather her wits and follow him to the children's area. Francie and Franklyn were the last two children left with the worker. Sensing that they needed time alone together, the older woman said a sweet good-bye to the twins before hurrying away.

"We tole everybody." Francie's chin jutted out as if she were ready for a fight.

"You told them Adele and I are getting married." Mac's gentle voice held no recriminations. He sat down on the floor in front of the two children and nodded. "But that isn't true, so do you think that was the right thing to do?"

Franklyn hung his head, but Francie was not so easily deterred.

"Yep, 'cause you and Delly love each other, don't cha?"

Adele gulped. And there it was. The truth as plain as a four-year-old child could make it. She did love Mac. But—

"We do love each other, sweetheart." Mac leaned forward to push the curls away from Francie's face. He cupped his hand against her cheek, his eyes brimming with the same tenderness that infused his words. "We love each other very much."

Adele's heart stopped. Mac loved her? Joy billowed inside.

"As friends, Francie."

And like a pricked balloon, Adele's joy collapsed.

"Delly and I have been very good friends for a long time, since before you and Franklyn were even born." He smiled as Francie's eyes grew huge. "We care about each other very much, honey, but not in the way married people need to care. That's a special kind of love. It's much different than friendship."

Was it really? Adele thought about Victoria and Ben. They were best friends. They cared for and depended on each other. They shared good times and bad just like other couples in the church did. Love hadn't worked for her parents nor for her. But she was beginning to accept that it did work for some people.

If she took a chance, could love work for her?

"Not everybody gets to share love like your parents, Francie. Delly and I love each other as friends, but we don't love each other enough to get married."

And there she had it, Adele decided ruefully, feeling suddenly bereft, as if she'd had a chance to grab a precious gift and missed. Even if she was willing to take a chance on love, Mac had just said he didn't love her. Not romantically. Why? Because she wasn't the kind of woman a man committed to for life?

"Did you have anything to add, Adele?" Mac's quiet question drew her from her introspection. Worry darkened Francie's eyes.

"I need to make sure you and Franklyn understand this, Francie. Mac and I are not getting married. We're not going to be a family with him. Francie and Franklyn and me— that will be our family. Period." She paused and glanced at Mac, who nodded his encouragement. "I know you guys want more, but that's the best I can do."

"But—"

Adele shook her head, inhaled and plunged ahead.

"If my kind of family isn't enough for you, Francie, if you and Franklyn must have a family with a mom *and* a dad, then I'm sorry but I can't adopt you."

"Then we couldn't live at The Haven no more," Franklyn muttered, head bent.

"I guess not." Adele wouldn't pretend the twins could remain because she knew that when their care worker realized adoption was out, she might transfer them somewhere else. The thought of losing these two precious kids made her heart ache, but to prolong the misery, to keep trying to parent when she'd never be their mom would break her heart.

"So?" Mac nudged when neither child spoke for several long minutes.

"You couldn't find us a different daddy?" The beseeching in Francie's glossy eyes begged Adele to reconsider. But pretending life was perfect when it wasn't? She'd been doing that for years. It didn't work. Slowly she shook her head. "I'm sorry."

"I won't be your daddy," Mac crooned in such a tender voice. "But I'll still be around. And I'll love you and care about you forever, no matter what happens."

"Sure?" Franklyn's question conveyed a tinge of desperation.

"Positive." Mac shook his head. "You won't be able to get rid of me."

But there was a tremor in the words that made Adele scrutinize him. *He really loves Francie and Franklyn*, she thought, amazed to see that love glowing in his aqua eyes. Mac truly means to be here for them.

And for me?

"I guess it's okay," Francie said after the two children shared a glance.

"You mean you want me to adopt you so we can be a family?" Adele clarified, thinking that it wasn't exactly a ringing endorsement of her bid for motherhood.

"Uh-huh." Franklyn nodded. "An' we won't lie no more," he said sternly to Francie.

"'Kay." The little girl stood. "Can we go eat? I'm hungry."

Mac's shout of laughter killed the tension in the room.

"Me, too," he told the kids as he, too, rose and shepherded everyone into the foyer. "Is it okay if I come for lunch?" he murmured to Adele.

"I'd like that." *Actually I'd like more than that.* She stifled the errant thought before it exploded into something she couldn't have. Instead she focused on securing the children in their car seats. But as she drove home, Adele knew she'd come to a turning point in her life.

Since the twins were now willing to be adopted, she was going to petition for an adoption hearing as soon as possible. Hopefully, when a date was set, she could talk Mac into coming with her because she was going to need a friend's support.

Somehow she'd learn to be content with his friendship.

"You know how to control that horse, Eddie. Now go ahead and do it." Mac watched the twelve-year-old take charge of his mount, a burst of satisfaction filling him that in a mere two days this kid had gone from scared and trembling to confident, at least when it came to his horse.

"You've done an amazing job with him." Adele stood at the fence rail, cheeks rosy from the cold, knitted hat covering her glorious hair, but her smile wide and as beaming as ever. Her red-gloved hands applauded. "Bravo, teacher Mac."

"It's not me, it's Eddie. He's finding his groove." In the two days since their temporary "engagement," Mac had tried to figure out why he felt so down. Adele was still his best friend, but it seemed like a barrier had come between them, and he knew why.

Gina.

The twins weren't the only ones who clung to Christmas dreams. At every opportunity Delly mentioned finding her sister before Christmas. And every time, guilt piled on Mac's conscience.

The only way to alleviate that burden was to find a way to give Adele the maybe-lead to Gina. Perhaps then the weight of guilt he constantly carried would lift just a little. He'd phoned again yesterday. This time a different person had answered and repeated that she didn't think there was anyone named Parker coming to the center.

Didn't think. He'd have to call again, make certain it was a false lead. Delly deserved that.

"Penny for your thoughts?"

"Not worth it." Mac was glad Adele couldn't read his mind. "Cold?"

"Nope, the joy of the Christmas season warms me." Her eyes widened. "Your mom and dad will soon be back."

"I guess. Slow him down a bit, Eddie," he called. "Don't want him to get too warm. You're doing great."

"How come Eddie gets special instructions?" she asked quietly.

"Because he goes back to Edmonton this evening and he needs some achievement, some progress to bolster him. Also, I have a hunch the foster home he's in is abusive." Mac pursed his lips, reminded again of the purple bruises he'd seen on the boy's back when he'd fallen off yesterday. "I'm going to ask Vic to get his social worker to check out his situation."

"You've really taken these kids under your wing. It's very generous of you to take such an interest in them." Adele sounded surprised and that bugged him.

"You didn't think I'd care if some bully took out his bad humor on a kid?" *What would Delly think if she knew how you've ignored Dave's emails, hung up when you heard his voice at the center? Neglected to respond to your former commanding officer's voice mails?*

"Naturally you'd care, Mac. You were always great with kids. I hope you have a ton of your own." Something on his face must have altered because she frowned and asked, "What did I say wrong?"

"Nothing." *I'll never be a dad.*

Change the subject.

"You looked pretty perky when you arrived," he said. "What's up?"

"We have six kids interested in your first daylong ski trip—next weekend if you're game." She laughed when he fist-pumped the cold air. "Didn't think we'd have any takers?"

"You're a good public relations agent, Delly." He couldn't smother his grin.

"I only reminded the last batch of kids of the fun they had at that rodeo you organized. They spread the word among their peers and voilà!" Suddenly her smile faded. "You're sure it won't be too much for you?"

"Nope. Gabe and I have it all planned out, with rest stops and lunches over campfires. I've gotten a lot stronger." Adele's face got a faraway look. "What are you thinking?"

"Just wishing Gina was here." She sighed. "Everything is so wonderful. Tons of kids are hearing about God's love and enjoying your ranch and The Haven. I want my sister to share in that."

"She'll show up one of these days," Mac assured her, squeezing her hand while his brain condemned him for not pursuing the one paltry lead he had. "Be patient."

"I guess. But I'm done being patient in another area." Her stunning smile stopped his breathing. "Remember I told you I was going to ask the kids' care worker to request an adoption hearing? Well, she did, and I got it."

Delly's amber eyes glittered with happiness. Her smile stretched all the way across her face. Even her voice oozed with joy. His heart thudded. This woman, this special woman reached in and grabbed his heart as no one ever had.

"Congratulations." Mac couldn't stop himself from bending so he could brush his lips against hers. "Mommy. Has a nice ring. What's the date?"

"That's why I came over when I should be baking Christmas cookies with Stella." Adele's face bore the same bemusement the twins had worn when they'd first gawked at his puppies. "I'm to meet the judge next Monday. Will you come with us, Mac?"

"Adele, are you sure?" He hated hesitating. He desperately wanted his best friend to be happy, but adoption was permanent, and he had this inner sense that Delly was making do, asking less from life than she truly wanted because—well, he wasn't sure why.

"I'm positive." Her smile melted, replaced by a frown. "You don't think I should adopt Francie and Franklyn."

"I didn't say that." After a nod at Gabe to take over with Eddie, Mac opened the gate and stepped out. He refastened the closure, trying to compose his thoughts. Finally, he laid his hand on her shoulder as if that would ease his words. "It's a lot of responsibility to take on, Adele, and you're already doing so much for The Haven. Plus, you're taking care of your aunties, and they're not young."

"They're not helpless, either. And when Gina comes, she'll help."

"You can't depend on that, Delly. You don't know if or when you'll find her."

Maybe she would if you ran that ad again, called the center again. Mac pushed away the nagging voice. Right now Gina wasn't his concern. Adele was.

"I will find my sister," she insisted.

"Yes, but— Listen to me, Adele." He exhaled before bluntly asserting, "You cannot start these proceedings unless you're absolutely certain about adoption."

"Of course I'm certain." She wrinkled her nose in confusion. "You sound like Rafe." She frowned. "He was positive I couldn't handle being a single mother, but I'll have my aunties, my foster sisters, the church, the community, my friends." Her smile flashed again. "It's going to be so perfect."

"No, it isn't, Adele. It isn't going to be perfect. There will be good times, but it's also going to be hard, demanding and sometimes thankless. There may come a time when you might even regret doing it. Are you prepared for that?" The words snapped out of Mac before he could stop them.

"I'll never regret it." Adele's blazing joy had drained away. "I'd hoped you'd take us to Edmonton on Monday, but don't worry, I won't bother you, Mac. Adopting the twins is all on me and that's *exactly* what I want." With tears rolling down her cheeks she stumbled away from him, got in her car and drove away.

Calling himself a fool, Mac returned to Eddie. Gabe left as he helped the boy dismount. Together they curried the horse. Once he'd taken Eddie back to The Haven, Mac went hunting for Adele. Time to mend fences.

"Have you seen her?" he asked Victoria.

"I don't know if I'm speaking to you, dream killer." Vic had always been protective of her foster sisters. "She was so happy she got a hearing scheduled. Why'd you ruin that, Mac? I thought you cared about Adele."

"I do care about her. She's my best friend. That's why I don't want her perfect dream blindsided by reality." He tilted his head to one side, waiting as Victoria considered that. "But I do need to apologize."

"Yes, you do." Victoria frowned. "Delly went for a walk. Down by the brook, I think."

Mac thanked her, about to take off on his search. But suddenly he had a better idea. He returned to his ranch and worked hard to get through his chores. Ignoring the reminder of those fragrant aromas he'd smelled earlier at The Haven, he ate some cold cereal and a banana for supper. Then he saddled two horses, riding one and leading the other, Adele's favorite, to The Haven. The softly falling snow made the woods a winter wonderland. Perfect for apologizing.

If she'd listen.

In the end, after he groveled, and with her aunts and sister urging her, Adele agreed to accompany him on a ride. But she said nothing as they plodded over puffs of snow, nothing when he lifted low-hanging spruce boughs for her to pass beneath, nothing when he stopped his mount beside the ice-covered stream.

"Can we stop here and talk?" he asked softly. "Please, Delly?"

"I don't have anything to say to you." She didn't look at him or accept his help as she dismounted.

"I'm sorry." Her sadness made him feel ashamed.

"Are you?" She did face him then, her amber eyes glinting like chips of topaz. "I thought that when I told you I was finally going to get my heart's desire, you'd be happy for me."

"I am happy for you." Mac slid his hand over hers and squeezed. "Happy and scared and worried and afraid and a thousand other things."

"Why are you scared and worried and afraid?" she asked, her face scrunched up with curiosity. "You don't trust me—"

"Just listen." He led her to *their* rock and waited until she was seated. Then he hunkered down in front of her and tried to explain. "You're taking on the raising of two orphaned kids who have been through a big loss. You're asking the court to give you permanent custody and *when*, not *if* they do," he emphasized, thinking what a perfect mother she'd make.

"Go on."

"When they do, you're going to have to nurse Francie and Franklyn through childhood illnesses, comfort them when other kids cause them pain, tend to their emotional needs, and a host of other duties—for the rest of your life." He paused to let those words sink in.

"I know." Instead of looking abashed she appeared thrilled. "So?"

"It won't be a fairy-tale, Adele, not the 'perfect' world you keep talking about. You won't be able to walk away when Francie and Franklyn get mad at you, or rebel and turn to someone else, or do something that might shame or embarrass you. Do you truly understand what you're taking on?"

"I'm not stupid," she said, forehead furrowed in a frown.

"No. You're smart and beautiful with a heart of gold. But I'm scared for you, Delly. All I hear you talk about is the joyful, happy side of adoption. I'm afraid you're not seeing the reality of this major step. You have to be prepared."

She kept her expression blank. Mac reached up to brush a strand of hair from her eyes, desperate to help her understand.

"You can't commit to these kids without expecting good and bad, Adele. It wouldn't be fair to them or to you."

"I'll be fine." The same stubborn toss of her chin irritated him.

"Your heart brims with love. That's the Delly I know and care about, my best friend." She was a lot more than that, but Mac wasn't getting sidetracked. "I couldn't stand to see you hurting."

Adele simply smiled confidently. Knowing there was nothing more he could say, Mac sighed and straightened.

"That's all I was trying to say this afternoon. That I want the very best for you."

Adele's eyes softened as she peered at him in the bit of light the shadowed moon offered. Then, to his utter surprise, she stood, reached out and hugged him. He caught his breath and slid his arm around her as a wave of yearning flooded him. If only he could hold her like this forever.

"You're the best friend a girl could have, Mac," she whispered in his ear. "Thank you."

He drew back, guilt suffusing him. If she knew…

"Don't say that." Mac eased away because it was too painful to remain so close to Adele and not kiss her the way he longed to. He desperately wanted to ask her to let him help her parent the twins, to love her the way he longed to. But he was equally afraid that if she knew who he really was, she'd have nothing to do with him.

"Thank you, Mac." The tenderness in Delly's voice was almost his undoing. "Thank you for caring enough, for being my best friend. You fuss and worry about all of us, don't you? It's nice to be cared for like that."

"My pleasure." He meant that sincerely. He liked caring for this woman.

"You don't have to go to Edmonton, Mac. Victoria's taking us." Adele smiled her generous, trusting smile. "But I sure would appreciate your prayers."

"You have them. Always."

"Thanks, friend. And pray for Gina, too, please? I have to find her."

Yes, he was her friend, but Mac couldn't say anything about her sister. To do so would only compound his deceit, and Adele was all about truth.

Chapter Eleven

On Sunday night, Adele sat on the foot of the bed, watching as Victoria sipped the hot lemon and honey drink she'd prepared.

"You are in no shape to drive with us tomorrow," she said. "I'll phone Mac."

"You'd rather have him with you anyway," Victoria croaked, then coughed as if to add emphasis to her words.

"Why do you say that?" Adele frowned at her.

"Oh, look in the mirror, Adele! You are in love with Mac. It's clear to everyone but you." Exhausted, Victoria leaned back against her pillow and closed her eyes.

"I can't be." Adele glared when Victoria opened one eye, then arched her brows. "He's my best friend."

"Exactly."

"Anyway, you know how I feel about love, Vic. It ruins things. Everything seems wonderful and then the arguments and fighting start and pretty soon you detest each other." She crossed her arms over her chest. "I'm not going down that route with Mac."

"Judging by this afternoon's argument, you already have." Victoria's smile flickered before she groaned.

"He defended the twins for lying to me about breaking

that dish," Adele fumed, still raw from their argument. "He knows how I feel about honesty, yet he insisted I was making it too big a deal."

"You were. It was old and cracked and they didn't drop it on purpose. You made a mountain out of a molehill." Victoria sipped her drink then growled, "Don't you think it's time to grow up?"

Adele frowned at her. "Meaning?"

"Meaning you've clung to the excuse of your parents' miserable marriage for too long," her sister said bluntly. "Yes, they fought, and yes, they messed up your childhood. Yes, neither of them has found happiness despite their repeated marriages. But at least they're still trying to find love. Anyway, you haven't been in their home for eons. You got to come here, to live with a wonderful family, to love and be loved."

"But—"

"You were blessed, Adele. Why isn't that enough? Why can't you let go of the past and choose better for yourself?"

"Like Mac?" Adele bit her lip when her sister nodded. "I don't think I can do that, Vic." At her sister's enquiring look, she confessed, "I'm almost sure he's thinking about leaving."

"But the daylong ski trip is fully booked!"

"Oh, he'll finish that, but I doubt he'll plan more. And the events he's always done for each group on the final day—" She checked to see if Vic had fallen asleep.

"Yes?" Victoria pushed herself up in the bed.

"I overheard him tell Gabe that the group on the weekend before Christmas will be the last one. His parents will be home then. I suspect he'll have Christmas with them then announce he's leaving." Heart aching, she tried to stem the tears. "I can't love someone who's leaving, Vic.

I can't believe in love when he's never said one word about loving me."

"Does he have to say it?" Victoria's quiet tone was gentle. "Haven't you felt his tenderness with you, the way he always protects you, tries to ease your load, especially with the twins?"

"He's always loved kids," Adele mumbled.

"Mac loves you."

"Then why is he keeping secrets?" she blurted.

"What do you mean?" Victoria gaped.

"Every time I bring up Gina's name he freezes. When I ask about his time in the military it's the same. He shuts down. I'm so scared of ruining our friendship that I'm afraid to push him about it. Sometimes when I talk about the kids and building a family," she confessed as she dashed away a tear, "Mac gets very quiet. When he does finally speak, it's about something totally different. He's keeping a secret."

"Maybe he is." Vic shrugged. "It is the season, after all."

"It's not about Christmas," Adele muttered. "I like Mac, a lot. But…"

"You're afraid." Victoria pulled her Bible from the nightstand, opened it and held it out. "Read the highlighted verse."

"'Perfect love casteth out fear.'" She frowned. "You're saying I don't love Mac properly?"

"I'm saying love means trust. No offense, Adele, but you've got this thing about perfection." Victoria shrugged at her glare. "Well, you do."

"So?" Adele just wanted her to finish so she could leave and mourn her love for Mac in private.

"Sweetie, love *does not* mean everything will be perfect. Humans are not perfect. We mess up, argue, make mistakes. But if we're smart, we forget about those and get back to love because that's what makes life worth-while." Victoria snugged her covers up under her chin and yawned. "I guess you'll have to decide if loving Mac is worth trusting him."

"I already have an awful lot on my plate. This isn't exactly the perfect time to fall in love," Adele muttered.

Victoria croaked with laughter.

"Sister of my heart, one thing I've learned is that there never is a *perfect* time for love. But if it's God's will, any-time is the perfect time. Now let me sleep. We'll see if I can travel in the morning."

"Doubtful, but thanks. I love you."

"Back 'atcha, kid," Victoria murmured before her lashes fell.

Adele tiptoed out of the room, closed the door and went downstairs. To her surprise Mac was in the kitchen.

"Vic's pretty sick, isn't she?"

"She's not going anywhere tomorrow." Adele wished Mac would come, though he'd already made it clear he didn't want to. "We'll be fine. I've driven to Edmonton a hundred times before."

"With two little kids? To a court hearing?" Mac shook his head. "What time do you want to leave?"

"You'll come?" Ecstatic, Adele couldn't help grinning when he nodded. "You don't have to, but I'd love it if you came." She told him when she hoped to depart. "You never said much about your first ski trip yesterday, though the kids seemed thrilled. Was it a disaster?"

"No. It needs a few refinements, but Gabe and I can handle those." He paused, stared at his hands. "Uh, Delly, I know you're mad at me about the twins' lie about that dish, and you don't agree with what I said, but uh, I need to tell you about something else I did that you might not like."

Adele's nerves tightened. This didn't sound good.

Perfect love casts out fear.

It was time to trust God. She shoved her hands in her jeans pocket.

"Go ahead, Mac."

"I ran an ad in the *Edmonton Journal* and I tweeted the same thing. Asking about Gina."

"And?" Excitement filled her. *Please, God, at last?*

Do it. Now, before you chicken out. Give Delly honesty.

Mac had struggled with this for days and he was sick of it. He couldn't even consider telling his parents he'd buy their ranch if he didn't get rid of at least some of this cloying guilt.

He didn't know how he'd manage the fallout, but he had to tell Delly about Gina.

"I received a response that directed me to a youth center in Edmonton," he said quietly.

"She's in Edmonton?" Adele's eyes glowed with joy. "I'm finally going to find her?"

"Wait!" He shook his head. "I don't think that's going to happen, Delly. I phoned to ask but it wasn't encouraging. Doesn't sound like there's any Gina Parker there. They don't give much information over the phone."

"So we'll go there after the hearing." Her topaz eyes sparkled as she suddenly hugged him. A second later she quickly let go. "Thank you, Mac. We'll find my sister and this Christmas will be the most perfect ever."

"Delly," Mac cautioned. "Your Gina probably isn't there but even if she is, she might not want to come here. Or there could be other barriers to this reunion you want so much. Please, don't get your hopes up until you've checked it out. I don't want you to be heartbroken if this turns out badly."

"Tonight the twins were asking me about God's love."

Adele's smile wasn't wholehearted. "They wanted to know if He would take me away like He did their other mother."

"They always ask the hard stuff." He smiled, recalling the flood of questions with which they always bombarded him.

"The bottom line seems to be that they're afraid to trust God." She smiled but it didn't erase her troubled expression. He loved that she was so concerned about Francie's and Franklyn's happiness.

"Lots of adults in the same boat," he said, wondering why she looked so sad.

"Including me. I'm assuming that this hearing is God's way of giving His approval for my bid at single parenthood but—" She shook her head. "I'm not sure, Mac. You and everyone else keeps warning me about how hard it's going to be, and I ask myself if I can handle it."

He'd never seen her so uncertain. And he hated it. This wasn't the real Adele, the woman who grabbed life by the horns and made something wonderful out of it. This was a woman he'd scared into thinking she didn't have what it took when it came to motherhood, and nothing could be further from the truth. *Fix it*, Mac's brain demanded.

"Listen to me," he said gently, moving in front of her so he could grasp her shoulder. "I know I warned you and maybe I said too much. There's only one question you have to ask yourself, Delly. Do you love the twins enough to stick with them no matter what?"

"You mean like 'for better or for worse, in sickness and in health?'" she teased, rallying to smile at him.

"That's exactly what I mean." He waited a moment, watched her eyes narrow, her lips purse, her forehead pleat. "Well?"

"I do," she whispered. "I love them with my whole heart, no matter what."

"Remember what the pastor said last week. Love is from God. So He gave you love for Francie and Franklyn. That's what you have to hang on to when things get tough." Mac could have stared into her eyes forever.

He'd never known anyone more beautiful, inside and out, and right now he wanted to fold her close and tell her how much she meant to him. But guilt lay between them. He'd only told her part of his truth.

"Thank you, Mac," she whispered.

"If God doesn't want the twins to be yours He'll make sure it doesn't happen. Because we know that 'all things—'"

"'—work together for good to them that love God, to them who are the called according to His purpose,'" she recited, her smile wide. "Yes. Thank you for reminding me, Mac."

Then she stood on tiptoe and pressed her lips against his. Taken unaware and unable to suppress his yearning to show this special lady how much he cared for her, Mac kissed her back, deeply, thoroughly, finally pulling away when she shifted her lips from his.

"Why did you kiss me?" he demanded when he'd caught his breath, while his eyes devoured her beautiful face.

"I thought it was you kissing me," she whispered. Then she pointed upward to the little sprig of mistletoe hanging above them.

Was that her only reason? Mac stared into her face, loving every familiar feature. He desperately wanted Adele to get complete custody of the twins. He also wanted her to have the joyous reunion with Gina that she dreamed of. But if he accompanied Adele to the center, they'd probably meet up with Dave, the truth would finally emerge and Adele would hate him.

So be it. Mac would do anything for this woman, including help her find the sister she'd longed for. No matter the cost. Because he loved her, and that was enough to make the consequences acceptable to him.

"I need to get home," he murmured, hating to let go of her, hating the chill that drifted between them when he stepped back. "I'll see you early tomorrow morning."

"Thank you, Mac. Friend," she whispered.

Friend. As he drove back to the Double M, Mac was completely aware that this might be the last time he left The Haven with Adele's smile tucked next to his heart.

"I don't have the right to ask You to fix my mistake," he murmured as he fed the minis and completed the other chores he'd promised Gabe he'd attend to. "I don't deserve anything. But Adele loves those kids with her whole heart. Please, God, please let the adoption go through."

Finished with his chores, Mac stood in the cold air, looking upward. He saw only dark roiling clouds obscuring the moon and stars. Perhaps it was a portent of things to come. The threat of tomorrow and the shame it would bring made for a very restless night.

"I'm so relieved it's not storming or anything. I don't think I could stand it if we had to cancel today's appointment."

Mac made no response and Adele didn't seem to need one. She, Francie and Franklyn had been chattering like magpies for most of the two hours they'd been on the road. In a way it was a relief he didn't have to make conversation, though his thoughts were not cheering. It felt like he was counting down the minutes until Adele told him she was disgusted by his behavior.

Mac drove to the courthouse through Christmas shoppers' traffic and found a parking place. After freshening up, he and Adele shepherded the twins to the informal room where the hearing got underway immediately. Francie was called first to speak to the judge.

Mac couldn't suppress a smile as the little girl wiggled in the leather chair until she was comfortable. Then she beamed at the judge. Adele's icy fingers slid beneath his. Surprised, he closed his hand over hers and whispered, "She'll do fine."

"It's not Francie I'm worried about," Adele responded with a grimace.

"We've prayed," he reminded. "*All things work together*, remember?" She nodded, squeezed his hand and seemed to relax.

Both the twins answered all questions put to them, though they digressed several times to ask the judge if he had children and if he liked to make Christmas cookies with them. The interviews ended on a shout of laughter from the judge as Franklyn repeated one of his knock-knock jokes. In Mac's opinion it had gone very well.

Moments later a court assistant ushered the twins from the room while Adele was questioned. Mac could see how nervous she was, but he could also see on her face and hear in her voice her love for the sweet twins and her joy at living with them as she eagerly responded to the interrogation.

"I love Francie and Franklyn. I don't think I could be prouder of them or love them any more than I already do. I believe they love me, too," she said as tears formed in her eyes.

"And if you are not permitted to adopt them?" the judge queried.

"That love won't change. I'll keep in contact with them, encourage them to be part of whatever family they are given. But I will always feel that Francie and Franklyn are my children, a very special part of my family," she whispered.

Mac had intended to pray for Adele through her interview, but instead found himself riveted by her excited voice as she relayed the list of plans she had for her future with the children. He found himself yearning to be part of it, to share every one of the precious milestones ahead with her.

Once you visit the center, it's over, his conscience reminded. *Delly won't want you to be part of her family when she knows what you've done.*

Mac snapped back to attention as the judge asked, "If you marry, Miss Parker? If you have your own children? What happens to the twins? What happens to your family dream then?"

"I—uh, don't foresee that happening, sir." Delly glanced at Mac. Her gaze skittered away. It returned a moment later, her eyes holding his as her amber irises intensified to a burnished-copper tone. "For many years I've believed marriage isn't for me."

"Because?" The judge leaned forward, his interest obvious.

"I come from a terrible home situation. My sister and I were caught between my parents' vicious fights. We felt like abused pawns as our family was torn apart. Neither of them seemed to notice or care what they were doing to us. My sister and I lost touch when we were taken into foster care. We haven't seen each other for a very long time."

"That's sad, but that's your parents' failure. Not yours." The judge frowned.

"I've had my own failures in the romance department, sir." Delly cleared her throat. "I was engaged a short time ago, for the second time."

Mac straightened. Second? He hadn't known that. Why hadn't Delly told him?

"In both cases I trusted wrongly and my relationships soured. I realized I was treading the same path as my parents." She looked directly at the judge. "I never want any child to go through what I did so I decided that marriage is not for me, despite the dream of happily-ever-after that every little girl cherishes."

"But you're not a child any longer. And you said you had wonderful foster parents in your aunts, that you've been very happy." He waited for her explanation.

"I am, more so every day. My aunts have made my life something to be envied. That's what I want to do for Francie and Franklyn," she said.

"And because your aunts never married, you think you can't?" Judge Barr looked troubled by that.

"No, sir. That is, I don't think that anymore. Thanks to my sister and her husband, and with the advice of a very good friend," she added with a smile at Mac, "I'm coming to realize that marriage is a wonderful gift from God that can be a strong partnership of respect and love where children flourish."

Mac felt the intensity of her stare as she looked at him. Time seemed to stand still.

"In fact, your honor, if the right man asked me, I would reconsider my stance on marriage. I believe love is something everyone should experience."

It felt like Adele was trying to tell him something. But what? Mac struggled to understand her unspoken message, but suddenly the connection between them broke as she looked at the judge.

"But only if the man loved Francie and Franklyn as I do. Then it would be per—" She stopped. Her eyes swiveled back to Mac, holding a bead on him, as if she was willing him to understand.

And suddenly Mac felt a light go off inside his head.

Had this woman, whom he'd known forever, just done a one-eighty on the topic of love?

"Please continue," Judge Barr said quietly.

"I was going to say perfect. But that's wrong," Adele quickly revised. "It wouldn't be perfect because relationships are never perfect. I'm learning that. But it would be wonderful."

"And so?" The judge raised one eyebrow.

"That hasn't happened yet. But Francie and Franklyn still need a home and a mother. I want to be that person." Adele's backbone straightened as she looked directly at the man who would decide her future. "Whatever the future holds for us, Judge, I promise to be the very best mother I can be. I love these children with all my heart."

"I thank you for your honesty, Miss Parker. I believe I have all I need to make a temporary judgment. Please wait here." Judge Barr gathered his papers then left the room.

"Well?" Adele turned to Mac and gripped his hand so tightly he winced. "What do you think he'll say?" she whispered though that was unnecessary, since they were the only two in the room.

"He'll say yes, of course. Where's your faith, Delly?" Mac eased his numb fingers from hers and flexed them, wondering if he should ask her to clarify her belief on love. But guilt held him back. "Thank you for mentioning me as one of your supporters," he said instead.

But his heart cried, *Friend? Is that all I can be to you, Delly?*

"You've never failed me yet, Mac," she said, her eyes glowing.

I will. Mac ignored the voice inside his head.

"I can't believe I heard you right about marriage." He searched her face, trying not to let hope grow. "Or was that just for the judge's benefit?" *Please say you meant it, Delly.*

"It was the truth. I no longer see marriage as I once did, Mac." Her smile seemed a bit introspective, even sad. "I think I was running away from love because I was afraid of being vulnerable. But it could be wonderful. With the right man."

Mac wanted to ask her more, to find out if Adele could think of him as the right man, as more than a good friend. But the twins' return prevented further discussion because they chattered nonstop about their tour of the courthouse with the judge's assistant. Their social worker, now speaking on her phone, gave Adele a thumbs-up before returning to her conversation. Mac opened his mouth to renew their discussion, but Judge Barr entered the room.

"First may I say I very much enjoyed meeting you, Francie and Franklyn. Thank you for telling me the truth. Sometimes that's hard to do."

"Welcome," Francie said. "Delly always makes us tell the truth. She 'sists on it."

"I think *Delly* does most things well, doesn't she?" he said with a smile at the twins.

"She makes the bestest cookies," Franklyn said, face serious. "If you don't gots none, maybe she'll send you some."

"Thank you. That's very kind." Judge Barr waited until Adele had shushed the children. Then he turned to her. "Miss Parker, I believe you have a huge capacity for love, already evidenced in your strong relationship with these wards of the court. You seem to have a solid faith in God and this appears to help instill values and consideration in the children. I already know your support community is very strong, which gives you resources to call upon should you need help parenting. You've clearly given thought to the future and the impact it might have on the three of you."

Mac's heartbeat stopped as the judge studied him for a long moment. Had he done something wrong, somehow jeopardized Delly's chance at custody? He heaved a sigh of relief when the magistrate continued his speech.

"I applaud you, Miss Parker, for coming through a difficult childhood with the determination and will to make the world better for someone less fortunate. Your work at The Haven is a testament to this." He stopped, consulted his notes, then continued. "I was pleased to hear that you're revising your opinions about love and marriage. Not all marriages end in disaster, though it does take commitment and perseverance to learn how to give your heart."

This time Mac felt the judge's scrutiny more intensely than ever. It took every nerve he had to remain in place, to meet the wise gray eyes and not move. Then the man shifted his gaze to Adele.

"I heard you use the word *perfect*. I agree that nothing is perfect, especially not love. But it is worth the risk." Judge Barr cleared his throat and stacked his papers against the table. "I hereby find Miss Adele Parker an excellent candidate for parenthood and award her temporary custody of the children for six months, at which time a second hearing will be held to determine permanent custody."

Mac couldn't swallow past the lump of joy in his throat.

"I wish you all a very Merry Christmas and look forward to seeing you in my chambers in six months. Thank you for finding this lovely guardian for these sweet children," he said to the social worker, then held out his hand to shake Franklyn's hand first, then Francie's, Adele's and finally Mac's. "Miss Parker must think very highly of you to allow you to be part of this proceeding. I hope you will honor that trust, sir."

"I will," Mac promised through parched lips. "Thank you, sir."

"You're welcome." The judge glanced from Mac to

Adele. "I look forward to our next visit." Then he hurried out of the room.

The social worker congratulated Adele, then also left. Alone with the kids, Mac studied Adele's face.

"Are you crying?" he asked, aghast at the sight of tears rolling down her cheeks.

"Did we do sumthin' bad?" Franklyn frowned.

"No. You did everything just right, sweetheart. You and Francie were great." Mac looked at Adele to see if she would tell them, but she was crying even harder, though she nodded at him as if to say, "Go ahead, tell them."

"Then why's Delly bawling?" Franklyn demanded, his face troubled.

"She's happy because you and your sister get to stay at The Haven with her. That's what the judge said." Mac loved seeing their faces light up.

"Forever 'n' ever." Francie's eyes closed. "An' ever," she whispered.

The judge's positive response made Mac think he didn't need to mention the next visit. But now even Franklyn looked like he'd start weeping. Mac had to do something.

"I think we should celebrate."

"With cake?" Francie's big eyes studied him. "It's not my birthday."

"No, honey." Mac hunkered down in front of her. "But it's the first day of your new family with Delly. She's your new mommy."

"C'n we call her that?" Franklyn sounded breathless. He looked at Adele and frowned. "She's still bawlin'." He asked worriedly, "Doesn't Delly want to be our new mom?"

"Oh, Franklyn, sweetie, I'm crying because that's what I want more than anything." Adele threw her arms around the little boy and hugged him close. She did the same with

Francie. "I love you two so much. I'm so happy," she bur-
bled as new tears flowed.

"It's okay, son." Mac wanted to shout with laughter at
Franklyn's confused expression. "Some people cry a lot
when they're happy, especially ladies."

Franklyn looked at Francie. They shrugged. "Weird,"
they said in unison.

"Yeah." Chuckling, Mac slid his arm around Delly's
waist and pulled her close. He brushed his lips against
her cheek, loving the feel of her silken skin. He knew this
closeness wouldn't last, so he savored every precious moment. "Stop crying, sweetheart," he whispered when he
finally pulled back. He brushed his lips over hers in the
faintest caress, then pushed her golden curls behind her
ears. "Be happy. Celebrate. God answered your prayer.
Besides, your tears are scaring the twins. And me."

In a flash the old Delly was back, laughing joyously as
she stood on the tiptoes of her utterly impractical yet completely mesmerizing spike-heeled boots and kissed him.
Every nerve, thought and emotion in Mac responded. He
felt perfectly in tune with her, alive and more connected
to her than he'd ever been with anyone else. This was everything he wanted—no, she was everything he wanted.
And he never wanted it to end. Because he loved Adele.

"Excuse me. Personal displays of affection are not allowed in the courtroom."

The laughing voice of the judge's assistant permeated
the cloud that enveloped Mac. He drew back slowly, feeling like he'd just emerged from a fog.

"Mac was kissin' our new mommy," Francie chirped
in her high-pitched voice.

"So's he gonna be our new daddy?" Franklyn asked.

"Good question." The assistant grinned. "Why don't

you ask them? After you leave. We have another session in a few minutes."

As Mac helped Adele with her coat and buttoned Franklyn into his, he prayed he hadn't restarted the twins' obsession with finding a daddy. He ushered them outside, avoiding Adele's glance as he joked and teased with them all the way to the burger joint.

Every fiber of his being felt alive with the knowledge of his love. Adele was who he wanted to spend his life with, the woman he wanted to impress and court and love.

But she didn't know the truth yet.

His stomach lurched. Time to face the music.

Chapter Twelve

"Can we leave now?" Adele had managed about three bites of her hamburger, but there was no way she could choke down anymore.

Mac's kiss had knocked her world off-kilter. He'd kissed her like a man kissed a woman for whom he cared deeply. Then they'd left the courthouse and he'd changed dramatically. She wasn't sure why, only that Mac was pretending he was okay while behind that blasé mask he smothered something that scared her.

"You didn't eat much." He frowned at her almost-full plate.

"Too excited. Custody of the twins and now maybe I'll get to see my sister for the first time in over ten years." She gulped, hardly able to process all the emotions whistling through her.

"Remember, the women who answered said Gina Parker wasn't there. It might not happen, Delly. Don't get your hopes too high."

Too late. She was full of hope, especially after that hearing. She was going to be the kids' mom, though she dearly wished she didn't have to do it alone. Why couldn't

Mac see that he would be the perfect addition to their per-fect family?

"I guess we'd better get on with it." Mac's sour tone enhanced the niggling worry that nestled inside her. "But you and I need to have a conversation first."

"About what?" Adele asked, but in the confusion of paying the bill and getting Francie and Franklyn out to Mac's truck and belted in, he didn't respond. She waited until he'd started the truck then laid her hand over his. "What's wrong, Mac?"

Tiny muscles in his jaw worked as he held her gaze. He seemed to struggle for the right words.

"Why are we stopped?" Franklyn demanded.

"I wanna go," Francie whined.

Heaving a sigh of pure frustration, Mac shifted into Drive and left the parking lot. He drove as if he knew where he was going, his face tight with tension.

"You know where this center is?" Adele asked.

"Looked up the address."

Something certainly was wrong, and no matter how she tried to pray, Adele couldn't stifle her worry. On top of that, the twins kept plying her with questions, leaving no time for her to find out what was up with Mac. By the time they pulled in to the parking lot of a former school that had a big sign out front identifying the building as the Edmonton Center for Youth, Adele's apprehension was full-blown.

"They're fussing," Mac said in a low voice. "Why don't you go inside and ask about Gina while I keep them busy out here?"

"Go in alone?" she asked aghast, her voice squeaky. "No! You were the one who found this place. You should be with me, Mac." She turned in her seat and said loudly, "You two behave."

Immediately the twins settled.

"Let's go in," Adele said, though she could tell it was the last thing Mac wanted to do. She had no idea why that would be, only that something was very wrong. They straggled across the lot, into the brick building and followed the sign to reception.

Mac said nothing the entire time. But Adele saw his hand clench and unclench. Maybe he was worried for her, lest they find disappointment. She stepped close to him and bunted him with her shoulder.

"Relax, Mac. Even if we don't find Gina, it's been a stellar day."

He nodded but didn't crack a smile.

"May I help you?" a woman behind the counter asked.

"Perhaps. I am trying to find out if Gina Parker is here. She's my sister. I haven't seen her for many years and I've missed her so much." Adele paused when her voice cracked.

"We do have a Gina working here. But her last name isn't Parker."

"Oh." Dejected, Adele almost turned away. But then her aunties' favorite verse filled her brain. *"In all thy ways acknowledge him, and he shall direct thy paths."* She whispered a quick prayer for help, then faced the woman again. "Might we meet with her anyway? Maybe she has information about my sister."

"I guess. She's assisting another counselor now, though. They're leading a youth group." The woman smiled. "We always offer several youth sessions around the Christmas season. Youth seem to be so lost without family. Can you wait about fifteen minutes?"

Adele glanced at Mac, who rolled his eyes but nodded.

"We can wait," she said.

"Have a seat. There are coloring books and crayons in

the cupboard for the children. They're such cuties." The woman laughed as the twins shrugged their coats on the floor then settled down to color.

"Thank you." Adele took the chair next to Mac, who thrust out his feet but didn't look at her. "What's wrong?"

"Adele, I need to tell you something and you won't like it." He'd barely said the words when a group of teens burst out of a door and noisily made their way outside.

"The group is breaking up early. You can go in now. Through the same door those kids just came out of," the receptionist directed.

"Thank you." Adele rose, irritated that Mac didn't move with the same urgency. In fact, he seemed to be unmoving. Surely whatever he had to say could wait a few minutes. "I really need you with me," she whispered.

He sighed, gave her a look she couldn't translate, then finally shuffled to his feet.

"You're welcome to leave the kids here. I'll watch them," the woman offered. "It's a slow day for me and I love kids." She emerged from behind the desk and hunkered down beside the twins, grabbing a crayon to join them. "I don't have any grandchildren," she explained with a laugh. "Go ahead and don't worry. We'll be fine."

A policewoman entered. The receptionist smiled.

"I was hoping you'd drop in. I just made a fresh pot of coffee. Help yourself, Sergeant Jones." She giggled at the sergeant's surprised look. "We're having a coloring party here."

"I'll stay here," Mac insisted.

"Please, Mac. I need you," Adele begged. "The kids will be okay with a policewoman here."

"Yes, they will. But leave the door ajar so you can see us while you're talking to Gina, if that helps," the receptionist suggested.

"Thank you. That's very kind of you. I'm a nervous new mom." Adele looped her arm through Mac's. "Come on."

The doors led to a gymnasium. A group of chairs formed a circle around two figures. Adele saw bright red hair cascading in thick waves around a freckled face she'd never forgotten, though it had matured.

"Gina!" she cried and raced over to the sister who'd been missing from her life way too long.

"Adele?" Gina grabbed her, studied her for interminable moments before pulling her close. It was enough for Adele to just savor her sister's embrace and let the past go along with all the longing and fears.

But her questions wouldn't be silenced.

"This is my best friend, Mac," she said, unaware that until then he'd hung back. "I've been trying to find you forever. Where have you been?"

"Australia. I moved there with my adoptive family. I only came back to Canada two months ago because my adoptive parents died in a car accident and I was all alone." Tears rolled down her sister's freckled face as she studied Adele. "When I learned I was moving there I asked, but our mom and dad refused to let me contact you. They said it would upset you too much. I'm pretty sure my letters to you got thrown out."

"I never got them," Adele whispered, heartbroken at the suffering she'd endured.

"I've missed you, Adele." Gina sniffled through her tears and explained, "I came back here, to this place, because before I was adopted, I ran away from foster care. This center is where I felt safe. My adopted dad was the counselor here back then. He helped me get out of street life. He and his wife adopted me. I'm Gina Jones now."

"That's why I couldn't find you," Adele murmured. "I

asked about you, but Mom and Dad both made up excuses about you being far away, too busy to bother with us."

"Absolutely untrue." Gina related the horror of her life after she'd been placed in foster care. Adele began to realize that her sister had suffered far more than she, and yet since then, she, too, had found a faith in God that had kept her grounded all these years.

"So you came back to Edmonton." Adele smiled. "I'm so glad."

"Me, too. I have my psychology degree now. I came here hoping to pass forward some of the blessings I've received. Dave's trying to do the same, so we're working together to help kids." She smiled at the man in a wheelchair beside her. "Dave, this is my sister, Adele."

"Hi, Adele." The big burly man grinned and waggled a hand.

"Nice to meet you, Dave. And this is my friend, Mac—" Adele glanced around surprised that Mac had retreated to the entry.

"Mac McDowell." Dave's greeting sounded guarded. He waited until Mac joined them, face inscrutable. "How are you?"

"I should be asking you that and I should have done it ages ago. I apologize, Dave." Mac seemed tentative, something Adele hasn't seen before. His quiet "How are you?" confused her even further.

"I'm in this chair. How do you think I am?"

Whoa! Adele blinked. Mac hadn't wanted to come in here—was this why?

"I'm sorry, Dave. I'd do anything I could to change that." Mac sounded contrite. "I know it's my fault you're there."

"Yeah, it is. You pushed that jet too hard, Mac." Dave's icy words scared Adele but all she could do was listen.

"They told you to ease down on the throttle when you hit that ceiling and you didn't."

"No, I didn't. The engine stalled and we crashed." Mac didn't sound like himself, not strong and confident. He sounded—ashamed. "I'm sure you hate me."

"I did," Dave said, eyes glittering.

"I'm not surprised," Mac muttered. "When I think about that day, I hate me, too."

Adele glanced at Gina, but her attention was focused on Dave.

"But what good does hating do?" Dave's piercing gaze searched Mac's.

"Dave was your copilot?" Adele frowned.

"And best friend, I thought." Dave still studied Mac. "He was my captain until we crashed. And then I never saw him again."

"I saw you. As soon as I was mobile, I went to the hospital. But I couldn't go in. I was too ashamed," Mac murmured. "Seeing what I'd done to you—" He shook his head, his voice choked. "I am so sorry."

"Thank you for saying that." Dave's voice eased. "But you lost something, too. Can't be easy for you."

"I didn't get what I deserved," Mac growled.

"Who does? If we got what we deserved, the two of us would be dead." Dave smiled at Adele's confusion. "I'm guessing this guy never told you he and I were the aces on our team."

"No," she whispered.

"Mac never met an aircraft he couldn't tease into a better performance. They gave him a medal because our crash revealed a fatal flaw in the engine. He knew there was something wrong and he wouldn't let it go, even though he disobeyed orders."

"I saw the medal." Adele glanced at Mac's frozen expression. What was wrong with him?

"I egged him on. Faster, higher, more. We were quite a pair and we both paid for our foolhardiness." Dave motioned to his wheelchair. "But we survived. Must have been because God had something else in mind for us."

Adele wasn't sure what he meant. Mac had always dodged questions about the accident. He'd spoken often about struggling to figure out God's plan. She studied him now and saw anger filling his face.

"I haven't paid nearly enough," Mac grated.

"You returned to that ranch you used to talk about all the time. Going home's good. Helping foster kids is even better." Dave's gentle tone surprised Adele. "Our center is part of the riding program at the Double M ranch."

"Mac's ranch? I didn't know that." Adele couldn't wrap her mind around it.

"We've sent several kids there." Dave kept a bead on Mac. "Eddie's the one who's gone through the biggest change. Because of the interest you took in him. You cared enough to question his bruises and now that nervous, uncertain, scared little kid is out of his abusive foster home. You teaching him to ride gave him confidence, Mac."

"That's exactly what my aunts hoped for when they came up with the refuge idea for The Haven." Worried when the two men kept staring at each other, Adele explained about her foster aunts, The Haven and their new program for foster youth.

"So when Dave was sending kids to the riding program, he was sending them to where you live now, Adele?" Gina's eyes twinkled. "I want to hear more. And I want to meet whomever that is in reception, giggling."

"My kids." Adele soaked in the sight of her beloved sister, now within arm's reach. "When you decided to stay, why didn't you let me know you'd come back, Gina?"

"I had no idea where you were. I went to see both Mom and Dad a couple of times. But they're both drinking heavily and neither one was very coherent. Nobody at social services would answer my questions."

"Been there," Adele muttered.

"I've been praying to find you for ages. Then Dave had this idea to contact an old buddy of his who's now a private investigator. We thought he could suggest—"

"That's what I did," Mac blurted.

When he glanced at her Adele's skin prickled. Warning bells rang in her brain and they didn't sound like Christmas.

"I contacted Archie. He suggested running an ad in the paper to ask for information. I did and it directed me here. But they kept saying Gina Parker wasn't here."

"Oh, that explains it." Gina chuckled. "Tracy told me someone had called last week asking about a Gina."

"Last week?" Ice crawled up Adele's spine. "You knew last week that my sister might be here, and you didn't tell me then?"

"I didn't know she was here." But Mac's face flushed a dark incriminating red. "They said three times that there was no Gina Parker here," he reminded but Adele was furious.

"You didn't think that I'd want to know that? You didn't think I'd want to check for myself to see if *maybe* the sister I've been searching for as long as you've known me might be here?" she said clearly, enunciating every word. "I thought you were my friend, Mac. I thought you cared about me." Betrayal made those words a mockery. "Clearly I was wrong."

* * *

On a flight school rotation in England Mac had learned a new word—*gobsmacked*. It applied to Delly now. Her smile, her happiness, the joy he'd seen just an hour earlier—it had all vanished. Now she stared at him as if she had no idea who he was.

Everything Mac had feared was happening. Once again, he'd acted on a hunch, on instinct. Once again, he'd blown it.

"You lied to me, Mac." Adele glared at him with loathing.

"I didn't lie," he corrected.

"Well, you sure didn't tell the whole truth."

"I didn't want to disappoint you in case it wasn't your Gina," he muttered but Adele wasn't buying.

"You didn't want to tell me because—" Adele stopped. Then her eyes widened. "Because you knew Dave was here." She shot him a look of pure disgust before turning her back. "Come on, Gina, I'll introduce you to my kids." She pulled her sister toward the reception area where Francie and Franklyn waited.

Mac sagged. Delly hated him. And he loved her. How many mistakes could a guy make?

"You okay?" Dave frowned at him.

"No." Mac shoved Delly's reaction away and focused on Dave. "Why are you here?"

"I came after rehab. I was training to be a kids' counselor, but I couldn't afford the tuition. So I chucked it all and joined the military."

"I remember you told me you wanted to be a counselor, but—it was too expensive?" Mac thought a minute. "That's why you enlisted."

"Thought that dream was dead. Turns out it isn't. I only need to complete a practicum to finish my degree. Gina's helping me get that." Dave shrugged. "I love working with the kids who come here. They don't care that I'm in this chair, so neither do I. We've all got disabilities. It's just that sometimes they're hidden."

"Like mine. I was a coward. I can't apologize enough, Dave. I owed you better."

"There was a time when I wanted your apology," Dave murmured. "But now it doesn't matter."

That hurt. But running away wasn't an option. Whatever it cost Mac, he was going to see this through. "I'm sorry."

"I'm not. I'm glad you came." Dave rolled his chair closer, his voice quiet and very serious. "I've been wanting to talk to you since the accident, but I thought maybe you needed some space. I'm sorry you lost your hand."

"How can you say that?" Mac demanded, eaten up with guilt. "You're in that chair because of *me*. Me and my hunches—I'm to blame for the accident that crippled you. Why don't you thank me for that?" he said harshly.

"Mac, that isn't all—"

"I was so sure there was something wrong with that aircraft. I had to disobey, push it further, higher, faster than we were supposed to. I would have done anything to prove I was right. What a fool I was!"

"But a lot of good's come out of you pushing. More than you know." Dave sighed at his disbelief. "You never read my emails, did you?" When Mac shook his head, his friend frowned. "I wish you had. Our CO must have left you phone messages."

"Several. I erased them without listening." Mac shrugged at Dave's gasp. "I took enough of a dressing-down when I was active. I don't want to hear it again. Ever."

"What that crash revealed is why they awarded you a medal."

"Wrongly awarded and I'm giving it back. I don't deserve it. Meritorious Service Cross," Mac snapped in disgust. "My least meritorious service was that I broke the rules and that cost you your legs. They should have given you the medal."

"I wasn't the one pushing to figure out the engine problem," Dave said quietly. "That was your bugaboo. I just had to live with your nagging for months."

"Until I went too far. And look what it cost." Mac had never felt worse in his life. "I know it doesn't help, will never make anything better, but I am so sorry, Dave. I should have said that to you months ago. I apologize for what I did to you."

"Mac, I am exactly where I'm supposed to be."

"Huh?"

"You and I are very small cogs in God's sovereign plan." Dave pointed to a nearby chair. "Sit down, buddy. You and I need to talk."

There was nothing Mac wanted less. He didn't want to look at Dave's useless legs or the many scars on his arms. He sure didn't want to remember his buddy's screams of agony as the fire exploded around him, or the way he'd begged Mac to help him die. What Mac wanted was the black unconsciousness that had overcome him on that terrible day.

But he owed it to Dave to at least listen.

"If our plane hadn't crashed, I doubt I'd have come here or pursued my degree." His former copilot leaned back. "I'd never have realized that my work, my past and my experiences could help troubled kids, desperate kids."

"You're trying to make me feel better about my stupidity, just like you used to. Don't bother. I know I've been a jerk." In a horrible, draining way, it felt good to finally admit the truth. Mac wished he'd apologized to Dave months ago. Instead he'd grabbed at the military's offer of an out because of his lost hand.

"But—"

"They would have found the flaw eventually, Dave. I shouldn't have tried that last acceleration. I should have left it to someone else. I wish I could change things but—"

"Will you please shut up?"

Surprised, Mac jerked his head up to frown at his buddy.

"You haven't changed much, Mac." Dave grinned.

"Huh?" Mac didn't get it. He'd cut off all ties with his old military friends because he hated that most of the old group thought of him as a crack ace pilot, worthy of admiration. He didn't deserve that honor. "Why would I have changed?"

"I kinda hoped you'd learned that God uses everything that happens to us for good."

"How can you being in that chair be good?" Mac demanded, irritated by Dave's acceptance.

"I wish you'd at least glanced at the stuff our bosses have been flooding us with since the accident."

"What's the point of rehashing it?" Mac demanded.

"For one thing, you could have spared yourself the pain of walking around with so much guilt." Dave shook his head sadly. "I'm sorry you've gone through this, buddy."

"Why are *you* sorry?" Mac felt like he'd missed an important piece of life.

"Because the faulty engine wasn't the only finding from our accident, which you'd know if you'd read my emails or listened to the CO's messages."

Confused, Mac stared.

"Our accident wasn't a mistake. I believe God placed you in that pilot's seat for the exact reason that you would push the aircraft as hard as you did. And I believe we

crashed because God didn't want us to be blown to bits.
Because He has things for us to do."

Mac stared as Dave explained that not only was the
engine faulty, but that engineers had discovered several
months ago that under certain conditions it malfunctioned
and blew up.

"We crashed before that happened."

"Meaning—" Mac couldn't quite assimilate it.

"Read the emails," Dave ordered, then leaned forward.
"The bottom line is that you didn't lose your hand for
nothing, Mac. I'm not in this chair for nothing. Because
we crashed, servicemen and women using that aircraft
survive. They won't suddenly, inexplicably blow up." He
smiled. "If that wasn't enough, God has brought us into
a different place where we can serve Him. Yes, you disobeyed and we crashed, but He used that for good, for
both our good."

Mac let the words percolate in his head, felt them melt
some of his frustration at not knowing God's will.

"Because of the accident, I'm finishing my counseling
degree, so I can help troubled kids. I'd forgotten how much
I loved working with kids."

"I'm happy for you." Mac clapped Dave on his shoulder,
truly elated that his friend had found happiness.

"Thanks. But it's not just me. Ever consider maybe our
accident was also part of God's plan to redirect you?" Dave
tilted his head to one side, a quizzical look on his face.

"Not even once." Mac's thoughts flew over the past few
months, remembering the aunts' advice to take one step
at a time. Running the ranch, doing the trail riding—*that*
was God's plan for him?

From the other room, Adele's chiding voice to the twins
broke into his thoughts and cast a chilling pall of worry. He
still had to make her understand why he'd delayed telling

about Gina. That meant he'd have to reveal his cowardice. Mac shrank from disclosing his deepest flaws, but Adele was all about truth.

"I've thought about your new direction a lot, Mac." The intensity of Dave's stare didn't diminish. "I've heard how you're liaising with The Haven. I've seen the results you had with Eddie and others, heard about the care you show each of them, how you try to find something special to teach them so they all come away with a feeling of accomplishment. Could that be your ministry?"

Mac wasn't sure.

"Seems God's given you a side benefit of being home on that ranch you love."

"He has?" Mac frowned.

"Adele," Dave said rolling his eyes. "The childhood chum you never stopped blabbering about during all those fly hours we shared. That's God's doing, too." Dave's smirk gently mocked him. "You get to spend time with the lady you've always cared about, because of our accident. The Lord works in mysterious ways, my friend. Now, let's go get the ladies and have coffee. We've got a lot to catch up on."

Mac hadn't seen Dave for months. Though he longed to talk to Delly, to explain enough to erase her look of utter disappointment in him, he also wanted to hear how Dave had figured out God's will.

"Got time for a java?"

"Let's do it." Mac doubted Adele would object to a few more minutes with her sister. "Where?"

"Here. I just got a fancy new coffee machine." Dave led the way to his office, pausing only to explain the plan to the sisters. "Gina brought Christmas cookies. They're delicious."

"How do you know that?" she teased, following him down the aisle.

"Oops." Dave invited them into his office and began making coffee.

Mac silently studied Adele as she sat Francie and Franklyn on the floor beside a coffee table and produced juice boxes from their backpack. She didn't look at him, but she didn't have to. He'd known her long enough to know her smile was forced and her usual spunk diminished. She turned her back on him as she chatted with Gina.

Mac accepted his coffee with a heavy heart. Delly wouldn't forgive him anytime soon. He coaxed Dave to talk more about God's will. It would give him something to think about on what would probably be a long, chilly ride home.

Delly's anger at him wasn't exactly a surprise. Adele Parker didn't tolerate untruth. Ever.

That was one of the things Mac loved most about her. But love meant truth.

It was time Mac came clean about everything to this woman he loved.

And then what?

Chapter Thirteen

It was late by the time they left the city. The twins, tired after their long day and full of spaghetti dinner, now slept in the back seat of the truck. Their soft snores emphasized the silence in the cab until Adele couldn't keep quiet any longer.

"When did you intend to tell me about Gina?" A miasma of emotion whirled inside. She couldn't seem to right her badly shaken world.

"On the way here." Mac sounded hesitant.

"That's easy to say now," she accused.

"But it's true. You don't yet know the reason I didn't say anything."

In the dash lights he looked gaunt and for a moment she felt sorry for him. But Mac had lied to her about her sister's possible whereabouts when he knew how much finding Gina meant to her. There could be no excuse for that.

Couldn't there? The voice in her head inspired a flicker of guilt. *No* reason she could forgive him?

"It's all tied up with my crash." Mac's hand tightened on the wheel. His shoulders tensed, as though he was reliving the horror.

Adele wanted to reach out and comfort him. But she

couldn't. Mac no longer seemed like her best friend. Now a distance gaped between them that she wasn't sure could ever be healed.

"It doesn't matter." She wished she'd never started down this track. She'd thought she loved Mac. But how could she care about a man who deliberately lied to her?

"Please, just hear me out." Mac sounded desperate, but pride pushed away any tenderness she felt.

"Why? So you can rationalize your lie, or make up a new one? Why couldn't you be honest with me?"

"I couldn't be honest with myself." His grated words confused her.

"Meaning?" The sheer anguish flooding Mac's dash-illuminated face made her gulp.

"I caused the accident, Delly," he said hoarsely. "Dave's injuries are my fault."

She stared at him.

"One of the reasons I did so well in my job was because I'm a risk taker. Or I was," he corrected softly. "Every time I flew, I took too many risks, disobeyed orders, basically tried anything that would get me the attention I needed. And I needed a lot of attention."

"Because?" Adele wasn't sure where this was going, but she clung to the hope that his explanation would somehow absolve his dishonesty.

"I had so many doubts about leaving school, joining the military. Recklessness chased them away." He swallowed as if his throat was dry and he was desperate for a drink. "My buddies called me Ace. I had this sense when I flew, as if the plane talked to me. And I kept sensing something was wrong with the last jet. But I couldn't figure out what. So I took too many chances and Dave paid for it."

"Gina said you rescued him. She said that's what caused your injury." The loss of his hand and part of his arm was an *injury*? Adele mocked her understatement. "Dave told her that when you pulled him free of the wreckage, a part of the wing fell on you, severing your arm."

The visual image of it made her stomach queasy.

"That's what they told me in the hospital, too. I thought they were trying to make me feel better." Mac shrugged, lips pursed. "I don't remember that. All I remember are his screams. He was on fire, burning up right in front of me. The man who prayed for God's blessing before every flight, who constantly asked for God's will to be done—he was covered in jet fuel and he was dying. Because of me."

The disgust resonating through Mac's voice silenced Adele. She didn't know what to say, how to help him. But then the memory of years of yearning for her sister hardened her heart.

"That doesn't explain—"

"When I woke up four days later they'd amputated my hand and my arm. I had internal injuries, broken ribs, cuts, bruises and partial loss of memory." Mac's words came hard and fast, as if he pushed them out to avoid feeling. "But I was way better off than Dave."

"But he was very friendly. He doesn't seem to hold anything against you," she murmured.

"He should hate me. I thought he would. That's why—" He stopped, gulped.

"Why what?" That pause made Adele sit up and take notice.

"I never spoke to him after the accident. Not after I was released, not in the ten months since the crash. I never apologized or said I was sorry for ruining his life. Like a coward I ran home and hid." He glanced at her, his face set. "It's been eating at me for ages."

"You didn't visit him? But I thought you said Dave had been your best friend?"

"He was. That's how I treated my best friend." Loathing tinged Mac's voice. "You don't have to say it, Adele. I'm disgusted with myself."

"Then when you found out Dave was working at the same place as Gina—"

"The first time I called, the receptionist called him to the phone. I recognized his voice though we didn't speak." Mac turned his tortured eyes on her for a second, revealing his inner pain. "I couldn't tell him who was calling, Adele, not out of the blue without having said anything for months."

"So you hung up. And you never told me about the center or that my sister might be there?" Adele demanded.

"The woman said Gina Parker was not there," he mumbled half-heartedly.

"So you keep saying." She exhaled. "I'm sorry for the guilt you carry about Dave. I'm sure it's been awful for you. But, Mac—" There was no other way to put it. "You deliberately kept information from me that could have led me there sooner. Gina *was* there. It's the same as lying."

"I intended to ask Victoria to take you there, just to make sure." The way his chin tucked into his chest screamed guilty.

"Don't make it worse." Fury raced through her.

"I'm not." Mac glanced at her. "I *was* working up to telling you about the center today, but the twins—"

"That's the thing about deceit, Mac. It's always everyone else's fault. My parents blamed Gina and me for their lies and their fights and broken relationships. For everything that was wrong."

"Please, Delly. I didn't intend— You have to forgive me."

"I *have* to?" How could her best friend betray her, withhold information? "Why?"

"Because I love you."

Adele laughed. Actually it was more of a painful gulp than laughter. "No, you don't."

"I do love you." Mac pulled in to the driveway of The Haven, where the Christmas lights illuminated the house and yard like a welcoming embrace. He braked and shifted into Park before he turned to face her. "I love you, Adele," he said very quietly. "I think I have for a long time. I just didn't know it."

Adele stared into Mac's face. She saw the tiny scar at his hairline where he'd been injured in a bronc riding competition in eighth grade and the dimple at the corner of his mouth that peeked out whenever he teased her. She studied his hand on the wheel, strong, capable, generous, with the mark where she'd inadvertently caught him with her fishhook.

Mac was her best friend. He'd been with her through the good and bad. But when she gazed into those lake-water-blue eyes, she knew that what she had to do now would put an end to that friendship.

"I love you, too, Mac." He moved as if toward her, so she quickly resumed speaking. This was not the time to give in to weakness. "But I can't afford to love you."

"What?"

"People who love each other don't lie to one another, Mac." She glanced over her shoulder at the sleeping twins, reminding herself of her perfect dream. "I can't love someone who lives a lie to protect himself. Love means telling the truth, no matter what it costs you. You lied about Gina. I'd always be wondering if you were lying about something else."

"I'm not lying about loving you, Adele."

"Maybe not." But the way Mac shifted told her he was still holding something back. "But neither are you telling me the whole truth. What else are you keeping from me?"

"You want the whole truth?" He glared at her for several moments, then sagged, as if giving in. When he looked at her the pain in his glacial eyes stabbed straight to her heart. "My injuries— I can never have children, Adele. The accident I caused took care of that."

Stunned, she could only stare at him.

"That's your dream, isn't it? Having lots of kids, building that perfect family you always talk about. The perfect life, the perfect home, the perfect family." His sardonic smile hurt to look at. "I guess it's a good thing we don't have any future together."

"Why?" She was so upset she could barely assimilate what Mac was saying.

"Because I'm about as far from perfect as it gets, and perfection is what you're all about. Because you'd always be disappointed by me and my shortcomings. I don't think I could live with that, Delly."

Adele remained frozen in place as Mac got out, opened the rear door and began extricating Francie. She watched in the side mirror as he lovingly cradled her close, as if she was the most precious thing on earth. His lips brushed across her forehead when she stirred. Then Francie lifted her arms and threw them around his neck.

"I love you, Mac."

"I love you, too, Francie," he said.

Adele wanted to cry as he tenderly carried the little girl inside The Haven. She'd held on to her principles; she'd stuck to her demands for honesty. So why did she feel so bad?

Weary beyond belief on a day when she should have been dancing for joy, Adele got out of the cab and began unfastening Franklyn's seat belt.

"I've got him." Mac edged her out of the way and scooped up the little boy. "Hey, buddy. You're home at

The Haven. Soon you'll be asleep in your own bed," he promised in the most tender voice she'd ever heard Mac use. "Here we go now, son."

Mac walked to The Haven, cradling Franklyn against his chest, protecting him from the cool night air. Adele followed him all the way to the children's bedroom, where they both helped the drowsy twins don their pajamas and climb into bed. Mac tousled Franklyn's hair and squeezed his hand. He promised Francie that he'd take her for a ride on his minis soon. After pulling the covers to their chins and whispering good-night, he paused in the doorway, his eyes glossy as he studied the children. Then Mac turned and walked out of the room.

After a moment's hesitation, Adele rushed down the stairs to call him back, to thank him for taking them to the hearing. To say something.

But all she could see were his taillights disappearing in the dark.

"I can't love him," she whispered.

"Can't, sister mine? Or won't," Victoria asked from behind her.

"Oh, Vic. This should be the happiest day of my life," Adele wailed. "I got custody of the twins and I found Gina." She burst out bawling. "And I found out Mac lied to me."

Victoria drew her close and murmured soothing words, but all Adele could think was that now Mac would never hold her again.

I can't afford to love you.

Two days later Mac's parents returned.

And Adele's words still haunted him.

"Don't think too badly of her, Mac," Victoria urged as she waited for the last of the guests to finish their riding lesson. "Her dream of perfection has taken a tough hit and she's hurting."

"Hurting because of me, because I wasn't honest with her." He sighed, castigating himself for it yet knowing that did no one any good.

"Yeah. Why weren't you?" Victoria stared at him. "You and Delly have never had secrets."

Mac almost shook his head. But bottling things inside was the first mistake he'd made. He wasn't going to make it again.

"Have you got a minute?" he asked.

Victoria glanced toward the bus that would take her guests from the Double M to The Haven. No one waited to board yet, so she nodded and leaned against a fence rail as he told her the entire ugly story of his accident and his actions since.

"I'm sorry, Mac. So sorry. I don't know what else to say. But at least your persistence helped uncover problems." She patted his arm.

"Not much consolation there," he muttered.

"Christmas is only three days away. Maybe that will soften Adele's heart."

"She thinks I betrayed her," he muttered. "That's unforgiveable for someone who values truth and honesty as she does."

"There's also value in understanding and forgiveness." Victoria touched his arm, her eyes soft. "I'll keep praying, Mac."

"Thanks." He forced a smile. "I guess my stupidity hasn't been all bad."

"What's that mean?"

"I think I'm supposed to stay at the Double M. Maybe God will use me here." He kept his head averted, not wanting her to feel sorry for him. "I realize that with Adele angry at me, the riding program with The Haven might not work out anymore. But perhaps somewhere else—"

"Adele and your issues have nothing to do with our business arrangement," Victoria interrupted firmly. "This program you're running is reaching kids, helping them. That's the whole focus of The Haven's ministry. I'm not prepared to sacrifice something God is blessing so that you and Adele can avoid each other." She hugged him, then smiled. "The kids are coming. Time for me to drive them back. Don't be a stranger at The Haven, Mac. The aunts would miss you. So would I."

Mac nodded, touched by her words, though he had no intention of visiting The Haven any more than necessary. It was too painful to watch Adele deliberately ignore him.

"If You want me here, God," he prayed silently as he walked back to help Gabe with the horses, "then please give me some reassurance. I'm going to need that to get through Christmas."

Without seeing Adele, the day dragged, even though he needed to prepare for the daylong ski trip tomorrow. Mac reviewed every detail of that trip repeatedly. He packed and unpacked his knapsack four times, checked the weather report and spent more moments than necessary with his miniature horses.

But no matter what he did, he couldn't get his mind off Delly. How many evenings like this had they saddled up and ridden to their special rock, just to share the beauty of the valley? How many times had she tipped her head back, closed her eyes and let the snowflakes tumble onto her face before laughing with delight? Years of memories cascaded through his brain. He'd never imagined he'd come to love Adele so much when she'd first moved next door.

His phone chimed with a text. It was from Tillie and Margaret.

And we know that all things work together for good to them that love God, to them who are the called according to his purpose.

His purpose. Meaning God didn't want him to be with Adele? That He had other plans? Like what—loneliness? A sense of loss threatened as the phone chimed again. Mac had to smile at the familiar words.

Trust in the Lord with all thine heart; and lean not unto thine own understanding. In all thy ways acknowledge him, and he shall direct thy paths.

"Good advice, ladies," he murmured as he patted Esther's flanks then exited the paddock. He paused to sort through the words the aunts repeated so often.

"Okay, God. I came here to figure out Your will for me," he said as he held his face up and let the soft fluffy flakes kiss his cheeks. "I fell in love with Adele. I disappointed her. But I don't want to disappoint You. I'm here. I'm trusting You. Please direct my path. I will go where You lead me."

The words seemed to break the despair that had gripped him. Mac inhaled the fresh crisp air, allowing the oxygen to permeate his entire being. He'd done what he could, apologized to Adele, tried to repair the damage his mistakes had caused. He didn't know what else to do. Now he had to get on with his regular life and wait until God showed him otherwise.

Mac grimaced at the thought. He'd prefer a list of directions. But where was the trust in that?

Trust in the Lord. He would.

But he hoped and prayed God wouldn't lead him away from Adele, the friend he loved with his whole heart.

Chapter Fourteen

Two days before Christmas.

Adele forced herself to focus on serving breakfast to the excited youth who'd arrived the night before for today's ski excursion with Mac. Gina had driven six of them from the youth center in Edmonton, insisting she had to see The Haven, Adele's home.

Adele was glad her sister was here. Maybe if Gina kept her busy she wouldn't have to think about Mac and what he'd done.

Yeah, because you not thinking about him is possible, her brain mocked.

Mac was constantly in her thoughts. All night long she'd wondered, was he strong enough to take on this trek? Would his injuries act up? Did he miss her as much as she missed him?

"Delly, you're not listening," Francie complained.

That's because Mac walked in. Why can't I stop staring at him? Why does it feel like my heart's being torn apart when he stares at me with those sad eyes?

"What do you need, honey?" She bent down to the child's level to force her attention from the man who, despite everything, still held her heart.

"Me 'n' Franklyn want to go skiing with Mac, too."

"I'm sorry, sweetie. Not this time." Adele ignored their angry faces and refilled the bacon platter.

"You don't let us do nothin' with Mac no more," Franklyn muttered. "We were 'sposed to ride his minis. An' we wanted to see his Christmas tree."

"An' visit the puppies," Francie added in an accusatory tone.

"Another time maybe." She was still too raw from Mac's betrayal to take them to the Double M. And yet, here he was, standing in front of her, blocking her way from the kitchen to the dining room.

"Can I speak to you, Adele?" he asked after greeting the twins with a hug.

She sidestepped him to place a full platter on the dining room table, then returned.

"Children, go wash your hands. We have the Christmas concert practice at church this morning." As they scurried away, Adele lined up the packed lunches she'd prepared for the skiers. "I'm afraid I'm busy right now, Mac."

"You're always busy," he murmured very softly. "I wanted to apologize. Again."

She didn't want to look at him, but something made her. His lovely eyes were shadowed as they met hers.

"I made a mistake, Delly. I didn't mean to hurt you."

"But you did. You deliberately didn't tell me…"

"I was wrong. And I'm sorry." Mac shook his head. "I love you, Adele. How many times must I apologize before you'll forgive me?"

"That's the thing." She gulped, then blurted, "I don't think I can forgive and forget, Mac."

"Because I'm not perfect?" His face tightened. "Because I don't fit into your flawless world?"

Adele so did not want to have this conversation now, with people milling in and out of the kitchen.

"I'm sorry I messed up. It isn't the first time and it probably won't be the last." Mac's self-mocking smile made her heart ache. "I mess up a lot, Delly. That's who I am." He exhaled. "Maybe you're right not to forgive me. You said you love me, and I love you. But I doubt it would work between us."

That shocked her. "Why?"

"Because you want—you've always wanted perfection. I just want to love you, to share the good times and the bad." His face revealed none of the fun and sparkle she was used to. "I'm maimed, imperfect and I make mistakes, a lot. Love is all I have to offer." Mac paused, slowly scanned her face as if trying to preserve every feature. "I'm sorry that's not enough, Delly."

Then Mac turned and walked out the door.

Tears began a steady course down Adele's cheeks and there wasn't a thing she could do to stop them. The rising sun outside enhanced twinkling diamond sparkles atop the freshly fallen snow.

But in her heart, everything seemed dark.

Empty.

Alone.

Four hours into the ski trip, Mac called for a lunch break.

"The wind's accelerated." Mac leaned toward Gabe, anxious that the kids not overhear his concerns.

"And the sun's gone." Gabe inclined his head. "Those clouds are dumping snow to the west of us. Won't be long before we get it. What's your suggestion?"

"Let them finish lunch and then get out of this valley.

I don't like the looks of that snowpack on the north face," Mac said, grimly checking it out.

"I agree." Gabe's lips compressed. "If those clouds dump wet snow on it—" He didn't finish, simply shook his head. "There was nothing about a storm in the weather report this morning. Maybe we're doomsayers. Want me to take the lead?"

"Yes. You can go faster. The kids can keep up. I'm the one slowing us down." Mac sank onto a snowy boulder and rubbed his knee. "If worst comes to worst, leave me, Gabe. Get them to safety. They're what matters."

"Not leaving anyone, buddy," Gabe informed him gruffly. "Relax that leg and eat your lunch. I'm going to check out the kids."

"Thanks." Mac poured himself some hot chocolate from the thermos he'd prepared earlier and popped a pain reliever into his mouth.

"Might say a prayer or two while you're resting," Gabe suggested when a huge gust of wind whipped off the sides of the valley. "This could get ugly." He walked toward the kids.

Mac prayed for God's help and direction to get the kids back to The Haven through what he feared would be a nasty squall. He also prayed for Adele, that she'd find comfort, that she was safe, that God would give her and her sister a good reunion.

He closed his eyes, pictured her, blond head thrown back as she laughed at the twins' jokes. He saw her eyes misty with wonder the first time he'd kissed her, remembered her joy when the judge had awarded her six months' custody. His heart ached as the sweet memories flashed through his brain.

I don't think I can simply forgive and forget.

She couldn't. Some inner part of him had been fully

aware that by not telling her of his discovery of a possible lead to Gina, he was violating her rule of utter honesty. He understood that the way Delly made sense of her life was by following unspoken guidelines that kept her self-sufficient and, she hoped, immune from hurt.

He'd wished that in returning to The Haven, taking the first step toward adoption and allowing their relationship to grow beyond friendship, she'd begun to loosen her grip on control.

He'd been so wrong.

Lord, I need Your leading now more than ever. Without Delly in my life—

"Everybody up. Now! Let's go," Gabe called, urgency filling his voice.

Wrested from his musings, Mac blinked at the snowstorm that now obliterated the looming hills on either side of their valley. Knowledge kicked in.

"Wait!" He rummaged in his pack, pulled out a bright orange rope. "We walk in a line. Everybody hangs onto this rope. Do not let go of it." He moved quickly, urging the six youth to comply. "If we're moving too fast, yell. But do not let go."

"What's wrong?" one of the kids asked.

"It's time we got out of this valley," Mac told him before shooting Gabe a terse look. "Everyone have their whistle?" He checked, noted that each skier pulled out the whistle on a bungee cord that he'd attached to their inner jackets before they'd left The Haven. "You get in trouble, you blow it. You need help, you blow it. Got it?"

Faces serious now, they each nodded.

"Our goal is to get out of this valley as quickly as we can. We're going to push, so do your best to keep going, but don't take chances. We don't want anyone falling or otherwise getting hurt. Safely but rapidly, that's our motto. Are you good to go?"

They bellowed their agreement, obviously seeing this as yet another challenge. But Mac felt misgiving crawl up his spine when he saw zero reception on his phone. He carried a satellite phone, but it wasn't receiving now, either.

"Gabe, you lead," he shouted as the wind howled down the cliffs.

Mac wasn't sure how long they'd been at it when he heard the first soft gentle moan and then the growing rumble.

"Avalanche," he screamed. "Hold the rope and move right, to the cliff face."

Time seemed to move both fast and slow. He backed against the wall and wrapped both hands around the rope, pulling as hard as he could so that the skiers were drawn toward him. But then the rush of snow slammed into them and he felt himself sliding away from the rock and into the maelstrom of the avalanche.

"God, help us," he begged.

And then the snow buried him.

"How long will a rescue take?" Aunt Tillie's worried face revealed her distress. "Why can't we reach them by the satellite phone?"

"The storm is blocking reception. But Mac knows these mountains and valleys like the back of his hand," the search and rescue captain assured her. "Before his group left, he attached a GPS beacon to each skier and sent us the tracking information. We know exactly where they are, Miss Tillie."

"Then why—"

"We can't fly until the storm blows over, Miss Margaret," the man explained gently. "But what we can do is pray."

"Of course. And that's what we'll do. Excuse us." Tillie took Margaret's hand and the two left the room, their steps heavy as they mounted the stairs.

"Is Mac mad on you, Delly?" Francie demanded, her face scrunched up. "Is that why he don't come back? You shoulda said you're sorry."

"Yeah," Franklyn added. "Like we learned at Sunny school. God forgives us so we're s'posed to forgive, too. Only I dunno what you done wrong." He looked at Francie. "D'you?"

"Nope, but it musta been bad." The little girl peered out the window. "It's nighttime. Is Mac gonna sleep in the snow?"

"No." Adele gulped back the tears that had threatened since they'd learned that Mac and his group had been caught in an avalanche. "Mac's coming home. He'll be here soon."

She hoped.

"Come on, you two. I'm going to tell Grace a story and you can listen, too. It's all about love and forgiveness, the reasons we have Christmas." Victoria patted Adele's shoulder, offering comfort. "Don't give up on him," she ordered fiercely. "Mac's the kind of man you don't let go." Then she led the twins to the family room.

"Adele?" Her sister studied her with a frown. "What's wrong?"

"I messed up, Gina." Adele threw herself into her sister's arms and wept. "I let Mac go believing I'd never forgive him. But I love him." She burst into fresh tears as she explained what had happened and how cold she'd acted toward Mac.

"But if you love him—" Obviously confused, Gina

motioned her to sit. Then she poured them both a cup of coffee.

While she did, Adele thought about all the years she and Mac had shared, growing up together, leaning on each other. She recalled the day he'd appeared at the Haven's back door, minus his hand. She'd been so happy to see him. Had she started falling in love with him then? Or had that been happening from the first day she'd arrived here so long ago, the day he'd first introduced himself?

"Pride," she whispered. "It all revolves around my pride."

"Go on," Gina encouraged.

"You know how bad it was with Mom and Dad?" Adele waited for her nod. "When that social worker took us away I was devastated that they let us go without a question, that they never contacted us, that they didn't even care."

"Let it all go, Adele. You've kept this inside for too long."

"When nobody would tell me about you, when Mom and Dad didn't come for me, something inside me decided I was never going to let anyone hurt me again." She glanced at her sister. "I became one of the worst foster kids in the system. Self-reliance was my means of survival."

"If you didn't depend on them they couldn't disappoint you." Gina nodded. "That's why I took to the streets."

"My mantra was 'I don't need anyone.' Even when I came to The Haven," she admitted, ashamed, "I clung to control and self-reliance. I'd learned to play a part by then, pretending to be the daughter the aunties wanted." Tears rolled as the truth poured out. "The only one who always saw through my need for control was Mac."

"He let you be who you needed to be," Gina murmured. "Quite a friend."

"Yes." Adele sniffed. "Do you know he told me ages

ago that I spent more time trying to not be rejected than I did building relationships? He was right."

"Because?" Her sister waited, one eyebrow raised.

"Because if I trust, if I let go of the controls, if I don't make sure every single thing in my life is perfect—" Self-knowledge seeped in like a light growing steadily brighter as it illuminated her inner cave. "If everything's not perfect I'll get rejected just like Mom and Dad rejected us. And that means I won't get what I want." She lifted her head to gaze at Gina. "I'm afraid Mac won't love me enough."

"Enough for what?" Gina pressed.

"Enough to forgive me, enough to understand me, enough to love me no matter what." She laughed mirthlessly. "Isn't it ridiculous? I, the most imperfect person there is, the girl who was rejected by her own parents, am trying to guarantee perfection because I've convinced myself nobody can do what needs to be done as well as me."

"Oh, Adele." Gina covered her hand, her voice so gentle. "Trusting no one but yourself means you have to do it all. That's the opposite of trusting God."

"Pride." She nodded. "I let my pride cheat me of Mac's love because I will only accept perfection. As if *I'm* perfect. I've been so stupid," she cried as fresh tears fell.

"You're only stupid if you don't learn from your mistake." Gina handed her a tissue. "The answer is to ask for forgiveness and start trusting God, with everything. That's something I had to learn, am still learning."

Adele thought about it, vaguely aware that the search and rescue people and others who'd shown up to offer help were milling around. They didn't matter. The real truth mattered now.

"Honey, you want Mac to fit your pattern, but God made Mac as individually as He did you, with unique foibles and a fantastic personality. If you love him—" Gina grinned when Adele nodded forcefully "—then you must accept that Mac makes mistakes, which, I suggest, you do also, my dear sister." She added with another smile, "If God can forgive you, how dare you not forgive Mac?"

"Yes, I see that now. I've been so stupid."

"Not stupid. Just wounded by our past. But trusting God is the beginning of healing. And forgiving Mac lets you start with a clean slate. You don't have to do and be all. You only have to be the woman God wants you to be."

With a pat on her shoulder, Gina went to make fresh coffee for the waiting searchers. Adele sat, heartsore and ashamed. She silently asked God's forgiveness. The release of control felt light and joyful.

God would help Mac. She could trust that. God loved him more than she did. When the twins raced to her, weeping that Mac still hadn't been found, Adele comforted them, teaching them to trust God for Mac's safety. Finally she was no longer playing a part.

At the bedtime ritual with Francie and Franklyn, Adele spent a little longer on their prayers for Mac and the skiers. Then she went downstairs to wait. She was trusting God, but she wouldn't rest until Mac returned.

But of one thing Adele was certain. If God gave her a second chance at loving Mac, she'd grab it, flaws and all. *God is love*, she said to herself. Now she had to trust in that love.

Mac forced himself upward through the snow until precious oxygen filled his lungs. As the last of the daylight waned he saw Gabe helping others emerge from where they'd been buried. Thankfully the cliff had protected them. No one needed rescue and there seemed to be no injuries.

But as he surveyed their surroundings, Mac's heart

sank. Their way out of the valley was now blocked by a huge mound of fallen snow. In daylight they might be able to negotiate a way around it, but not in the dark. They were going to have to camp here overnight.

After conferring with Gabe, they found a small opening in the granite cliff and huddled inside around a fire of brush they gathered so everyone could keep warm. The snow still fell and the wind still blew, but here in this tiny hollow of the cliff they were protected. There were enough leftovers from lunch for everyone to eat something and the kids generously shared what little hot chocolate they had left in their flasks.

"I've got a couple of water bottles in my pack. You?" Mac asked Gabe quietly.

"The same. And some chocolate bars. Thought I'd save them for breakfast."

They discussed options.

"Let's get them to sleep if they can," Mac murmured. "They'll need their strength in the morning to ski out."

"They need something to calm them. Any ideas?"

"Story time?" Mac sat on a rock, his thoughts tumbling around. Those few moments, face buried in the snow, he'd accepted that although he loved Adele, God's plan for him might not include that.

He hated the thought, wanted to rail against it. He loved her. She loved him. Why couldn't… In the recesses of his mind, Mac heard the word *trust*. Trust in God's plan for his life? But what did that mean?

He knew. No more pretense or running away, which he now accepted was what his risk taking had always been about. Time to stay on the ranch, buy out his parents and get on with doing whatever God sent his way. He'd never have his own children; he might never have Adele to love, either. Though he hated that thought, he would let God work it out.

"All things work together for good to them that love God."

Never had the aunts' verse seemed more apropos. How blessed he'd been to have them in his life.

As Mac glanced around the group of youngsters who'd come on this trek to escape their troubled lives, certainty filled him. *This* was God's work for him. They were stranded and Mac's phone didn't work, but he wasn't depending on himself or a phone. He was depending on God. God wouldn't fail them.

"All things work together..."

Suddenly, above the crackle of the burning branches, with the world beyond the cave now completely dark, coyotes began to howl. The kids stared at each other, eyes wide with fear. Mac hesitated, unsure what to do next.

Okay, God. Help me calm them, let them know You are in control.

"You guys worried about that? Don't be. Coyotes like to howl. That's how they communicate. I've been listening to them do that for years. I grew up on a ranch next door to The Haven. Gabe works there, too. Coyotes are a fact of our lives, just like other problems."

Somehow the words came, the story of his childhood, Carter's death from brain cancer and his own need to run from life's complications. And then he told them why he didn't need to run anymore, how he'd realized that wherever he was, God was there, loving him, caring for him.

Frequently one of the youth would comment on something about his own life, draw a comparison or bring up a personal issue. Implicit in every remark was a plea for help, for understanding. And together Mac and Gabe strove to offer support, suggestions and always to draw the focus back to God's love for each of them.

When the last kid fell asleep, Mac took first watch. He sat, back to the fire, and peered into the darkness, watching as the storm finally died away and peace descended. Sometime after midnight the northern lights began their blue-green dance over the mountaintops, swirling and spinning like an eerie ballet in the sky. Mac's thoughts returned to Adele. He didn't know God's plan for her, only that He had one.

"Keep her and the twins safe. Comfort her heart. Let her know You love her."

Now Mac would wait until God worked things out.

Chapter Fifteen

The whir of helicopter blades wakened Adele on Christmas Eve morning. She pushed away from the table and ran to the door, throwing it wide open as the chopper landed, uncaring that she was blasted by snow and wind from the whirring blades.

"Please, God, let Mac be safe."

Search and rescue members rushed to the door of the machine and opened it. One by one the youth were helped from the helicopter, smiling and obviously thrilled with their ride back to The Haven.

Adele searched each face, desperate to see the one she loved. But as the last youth straggled toward her, only Gabe emerged, his face revealing his exhaustion. Oh, no. He was waving over the men with the ambulance. For Mac?

Uncaring that she hadn't combed her snarly hair or washed her face, or that she was wearing her rattiest robe and slippers, Adele burst from the house, racing past the startled youth toward the helicopter. Who cared what she looked like? It was Mac who mattered, Mac whom she adored and loved more than anything. And then she heard his voice coming from inside the chopper.

"I am *not* going to be carried out, Gabe. I can walk perfectly well. It's just a spasm."

"Mac?" Adele stopped at the door of the chopper and let her brain soak in all his beloved details. His face was haggard, his ski suit torn on one shoulder, and he was rubbing his leg. But he was here and he was alive.

Thank You, God.

"Hey, Delly. What's for breakfast?" Mac scooted forward and, with Gabe's assistance, stepped out of the chopper. "We're starved."

Adele couldn't have cared less who was watching or how she looked. She stepped forward, threw her arms around him and said, "I love you, Mac McDowell."

"Huh?" He stared at her, his meltwater-eyes wide. His hand lifted and touched her cheek in the most tender caress before he grinned and shook his head. "I think my hearing's gone. Could you say that again? Please?"

"I'll say it so often you'll get sick of it," she laughed. "I love you." Then she stood on her tiptoes and kissed him with every ounce of adoration that welled inside. And unbelievably, Mac kissed her back, his arm tight about her waist as if he'd never let her go.

"Uh, you folks want to take this show inside?" Gabe asked in a droll voice, barely concealing his mirth. "I, for one, am cold."

"You go ahead, buddy. We'll be there in a minute. I've got something to do first." Mac nodded his thanks as one of the rescue squad threw a blanket over his and Adele's shoulders before walking away. Then he tilted his head and kissed her again, more thoroughly this time, as if she was the most precious thing in his world.

"Mac, I'm sorry. I should never—" He placed a fingertip over her lips.

"I love you, Adele. More than anything. I'm sorry I didn't tell you about the center—"

"It doesn't matter, Mac," she interrupted. "All that matters is that I love you. You've always been my best friend. I don't ever want that to change."

"I do." He grinned. "I finally figured out God's plan for my life. He wants me here, well, on the Double M. With you, if you'll marry me. Together we'll be part of The Haven's ministry."

"And help troubled youth while we raise Franklyn and Francie. Yes, I will marry you." She giggled at his astounded look, then thrust out her hand. "I'm pretty sure that's God's plan for me, too. Do we have a deal?"

Mac frowned. "Your agreement feels a little—rushed. I might need some persuading."

"My dear man, I love you very much. But it's cold out here, my hair's a mess, I have on no makeup and—"

"To me you're the most beautiful woman in the world, Delly," Mac said gallantly before kissing her again.

"Thank you, darling. But my feet are freezing." She danced on the snow as if to demonstrate. "I know everybody's inside and they'll all be staring at us and smirking as if they already knew we loved each other, and I think I can stand that if you're by my side. But I have to make breakfast."

"Always practical Adele." With a shout of laughter, Mac kissed her once more, then hand in hand they raced to The Haven's back door and burst inside. Immediately everyone began to clap. Unabashed, Mac bowed.

"Thank you. And just so you know, Adele has agreed to marry me. We're going to buy out my folks and run the Double M while we work with The Haven's ministries."

"And we're going to have at least two children, Francie and Franklyn," Adele added. Then in front of Mac's parents, her aunts, Victoria and Ben, Gina, Gabe and Jake, the youth ski group, the rescuers, and her two children, she threw her arms around Mac and kissed him. "I'm so happy."

Francie nudged Franklyn. "I tole you God'd give us a daddy for Christmas."

"He's early. T'morrow's Christmas, silly." Franklyn frowned. "I'm starvin'. When's Delly gonna make breakfast?"

"I dunno." Francie frowned. "She an' Mac look dumb."

"I'm never gonna look dumb when I get old," Franklyn assured her.

"Me, neither."

Adele Parker's wedding to Mac McDowell took place at The Haven on New Year's Eve. The locals weren't surprised. The couple had known each other forever and with the twins' upcoming adoption it was understandable that neither wanted to wait. Tillie and Margaret issued an open invitation to the wedding, which meant The Haven was packed—exactly what the Spenser sisters hoped for.

At exactly 7 p.m., Adele's foster sisters and Gina, all wearing red velvet gowns with white feathered boa trim, led a procession down the stairs and into the family room. Flower girl Francie followed in a red sparkly dress that just grazed the tips of her new white patent shoes. Franklyn, wearing a dark suit and cowboy boots like Mac, walked beside her, carrying a white cushion with wedding rings tied on.

The bride descended the stairs looking beautiful in a chicly elegant white satin gown that emphasized her lovely figure and the sheaf of dark red roses she carried. At the bottom of the stairs, her aunts, Tillie and Margaret, took their place on either side to walk Adele to her groom. After kissing her cheek, they placed her hand in Mac's.

The groom's turquoise gaze, brimming with love, met Adele's.

"Are you sure, Delly?" he whispered.

"Uh-huh. You?" She held his gaze.

"Positive." There was no doubt in the words or on his face.

With the pastor's leading they repeated the vows that would join them together, pledging to honor each other and God, trusting Him with whatever their future brought.

Franklyn heaved a sigh of relief when the platinum bands were no longer his responsibility.

"Are me 'n Francie gonna marry somebody someday?" he asked Victoria as Mac slid the platinum circlet on Adele's finger.

"I hope so," she whispered.

"Do I gotta kiss some girl like Mac's kissin' Delly?" he asked, face screwed up in dismay.

"Trust me, sweetheart, when the time comes, you'll like it," she assured him with a loving glance at her husband, Ben.

"May I present to you, Mr. and Mrs. Mac McDowell. I hope you'll support and pray for them as they look to God for their future together," the pastor said.

"I love you, Mac." Adele had never felt more confident about love than now.

"I love you, too, Mrs. McDowell." Mac's gaze moved to the twins, then slid to her face. "You won't—"

"I'll rejoice in having whatever God gives me," she told him honestly. "It's all about trust, Mac."

"Perfect. Let's celebrate, my darling."

And celebrate they did, with friends and family. By the time the clock ticked down the last few minutes of the old year, Francie and Franklyn were asleep on the aunts' chairs in front of the fireplace, wedding cake icing and happy smiles on their faces.

Adele excused herself from some friends and found her groom. "You ready to leave soon?" she whispered, loving the way his arm curled around her waist.

"Right after midnight. We start our new life at The Haven and soon we'll leave for our honeymoon." He watched the clock as they counted down with everyone else. "Happy New Year, my darling Delly."

"Happy New Year, Mac." She savored his kiss, the first in a year that brimmed with promise. *Thank You, Lord. What more could I want?*

Half an hour later they'd changed and were almost out the door when the aunts called them back.

"There's a phone call," Tillie said, brow furrowed. "Someone called Enid insists on speaking to you."

"What could the twins' social worker want now?" Adele grabbed Mac's hand and held on, trying to prepare for bad news as she picked up the phone. "Hello?"

"Congratulations, Adele. I hear you're newly married. Sorry to interrupt the proceedings but I have a problem I hope you can help with."

"We were just leaving for Edmonton for our honeymoon, Enid." Adele clung to Mac's hand as her heart prayed.

"Then my timing's perfect. Can you call me tomorrow? I need someone to foster a newborn boy whose mother died today in a car crash. I know you are the perfect person for him."

"Oh, I'm far from perfect," Adele assured her as she tossed a smirk at Mac, who grinned. "But my husband and I would be delighted to foster this child. We are ready, willing and able to be used however God wants."

"Good. Call me tomorrow. Congratulations again and happy New Year!"

Adele hung up, her heart thrilling. She and Mac snuck out of the house and drove toward Edmonton.

"You're very quiet. What's going on in that lovely head?" he asked.

"I was just wondering. Do you think our life on the Double M and at The Haven with Francie and Franklyn and now fostering this little boy will be enough excitement for you?"

Mac pulled over, drew her close and kissed her. Then he laughed.

"My darling Delly, I'm positive that marriage to you, running the ranch, parenting the twins and whomever else God sends will provide all the excitement I'll ever need."

"Then everything will be perfect," she said.

"Absolutely perfect."

Then they drove off, toward their future.

* * * * *

*If you enjoyed this story, pick up the first
Rocky Mountain Haven book,*

Meant-to-Be Baby

and these other stories from Lois Richer:

The Rancher's Family Wish
Her Christmas Family Wish
The Cowboy's Easter Family Wish
The Twins' Family Wish
A Dad for Her Twins
Rancher Daddy
Gift-Wrapped Family
Accidental Dad

Available now from Love Inspired!

Find more great reads at www.LoveInspired.com

Dear Reader,

Welcome back to The Haven, a refuge hidden in the foothills of the Canadian Rockies where foster kids come to find hope.

I hope you've enjoyed Adele Parker's journey toward motherhood and love as she learns that God doesn't expect perfection. He expects our trust. After Mac lost his hand in an airplane crash he caused, his struggle to learn God's plan for his future got tied up with guilt. Mac doesn't get a list of "next steps" from God, but he, like Adele, learns that if he keeps seeking God's will, Our Father will point the way. As they travel that path, best friends Mac and Adele realize that friendship has changed to love.

I hope you'll visit The Haven again to read how grief and loss bring Olivia joy and love.

Until we meet again may you find abundant faith, infinite peace and the love that comes from God.

Blessings,

Get 4 FREE REWARDS!

We'll send you 2 FREE Books plus 2 FREE Mystery Gifts.

Love Inspired® books feature contemporary inspirational romances with Christian characters facing the challenges of life and love.

FREE
Value Over
$20

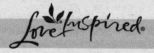
Rainbow Girl stepped into his field of vision from the kitchen area. *"Hallo."*

Eli's insides did funny things at the sight of her.

"Did you need something?"

He cleared his throat. "I came for a drink of water."

"Come on in." She pulled a glass out of the cupboard, filled it at the sink and handed it to him.

"Danki."

She gifted him with a smile. *"Bitte.* How's it going out there?"

He smiled back. "Fine." He gulped half the glass, then slowed down to sips. No sense rushing.

After a minute, she folded her arms. "Go ahead. Ask your question."

"What?"

"You obviously want to ask me something. What is it? Why do I color my hair all different colors? Why do I dress like this? Why did I leave? What is it?"

She posed all *gut* questions, but not the one he needed an answer to. A question that was no business of his to ask.

"Go ahead. Ask. I don't mind." Very un-Amish, but she'd offered. *Ne,* insisted.

He cleared his throat. "Are you going to stay?"

She stared for a moment, then looked away. Obviously not the question she'd expected, nor one she wanted to answer.

He'd made her uncomfortable. He never should have asked. What if she said *ne*? Did he want her to say *ja*? "You don't have to tell me." He didn't want to know anymore.

She pinned him with her steady brown gaze. "I don't know. I don't want to, but I'm sort of in a bind at the moment."

Maybe for the reason she'd been so sad the other day, which had made him feel sympathy for her.

He appreciated her honesty. "Then why does our bishop think you are?"

"He's hoping I do."

His heart tightened. "Why are you giving him false hope?" Why was she giving Eli false hope?

"I'm not. I've told him this is temporary. He won't listen. Maybe you could convince him to stop this foolishness—" she waved her hand toward where the building activity was going on "—before it's too late."

He chuckled. "You don't tell the bishop what to do. *He* tells you."

He really should head back outside to help the others. Instead, he filled his glass again and leaned against the counter. He studied her over the rim of his glass. Did he want Rainbow Girl to stay? She'd certainly turned things upside down around here. Turned him upside down. Instead of working in his forge—where he most enjoyed spending time—he was here, and gladly so. He preferred working with iron rather than wood, but today, carpentry strangely held more appeal.

Time to get back to work. He guzzled the rest of his water and set the glass in the sink. *"Danki."* As he turned to leave, something on the table caught his attention. The door knocker he'd made years ago for Dorcas—Rainbow Girl—ne, Dorcas, but now Rainbow Girl had it. They were the same person, but not the same. He crossed to the table and picked up his handiwork. "You kept this?"

She came up next to him. *"Ja.* I liked having a reminder of…"

"Of what?" Dare he hope him?

She stared at him. "Of…my life growing up here."

That was probably a better answer. He didn't need to be thinking of her as anything more than a lost *Englisher*.

Don't miss Courting Her Prodigal Heart *by Mary Davis,*
available January 2019 wherever
Love Inspired® books and ebooks are sold.

www.LoveInspired.com

Looking for inspiration in tales
of hope, faith and heartfelt romance?

Check out **Love Inspired**® and
Love Inspired® Suspense books!

New books available every month!

LIGENRE2018R2

SPECIAL EXCERPT FROM

Love Inspired
SUSPENSE

*With a price on his witness's head,
US marshal Jonathan Mast can think of only
one place to hide Celeste Alexander—in the
Amish community he left behind. But will this trip
home save their lives...and convince them that a
Plain life together is worth fighting for?*

*Read on for a sneak preview of
Amish Hideout by Maggie K. Black,
the exciting beginning to the Amish Witness Protection
miniseries, available January 2019
from Love Inspired Suspense!*

Time was running out for Celeste Alexander. Her fingers flew over the keyboard, knowing each keystroke could be her last before US marshal Jonathan Mast arrived to escort her to her new life in the witness protection program.

"You gave her a laptop?" US marshal Stacy Preston demanded. "Please tell me you didn't let her go online."

"Of course not! She had a basic tablet, with the internet capability disabled." US marshal Karl Adams shot back even before Stacy had finished her sentence.

The battery died. She groaned. Well, that was that.

"You guys mind if I go upstairs and get my charging cable?"

The room went black. Then she heard the distant sound of gunfire erupting outside.

"Get Celeste away from the windows!" Karl shouted. "I'll cover the front."

What was happening? She felt Stacy's strong hand on her arm pulling her out of her chair.

"Come on!" Stacy shouted. "We have to hurry—"

Her voice was swallowed up in the sound of an explosion, expanding and roaring around them, shattering the windows, tossing Celeste backward and engulfing the living room in smoke. Celeste hit the floor, rolled and hit a door frame. She crawled through it, trying to get away from the smoke billowing behind her.

Suddenly a strong hand grabbed her out of the darkness, taking her by the arm and pulling her up to her feet so sharply she stumbled backward into a small room. The door closed behind them. She opened her mouth to scream, but a second hand clamped over her mouth. A flashlight flickered on and she looked up through the smoky haze, past worn blue jeans and a leather jacket, to see the strong lines of a firm jaw trimmed with a black beard, a straight nose and serious eyes staring into hers.

"Celeste Alexander?" He flashed a badge. "I'm Marshal Jonathan Mast. Stay close. I'll keep you safe."

Don't miss
Amish Hideout *by Maggie K. Black,*
available January 2019 wherever
Love Inspired® Suspense books and ebooks are sold.

www.LoveInspired.com

Inspirational Romance to Warm Your Heart and Soul

Join our social communities to connect with other readers who share your love!

Sign up for the Love Inspired newsletter at **www.LoveInspired.com** to be the first to find out about upcoming titles, special promotions and exclusive content.

CONNECT WITH US AT:

Facebook.com/groups/HarlequinConnection

 Facebook.com/LoveInspiredBooks

 Twitter.com/LoveInspiredBks

LISOCIAL2018